"The job!" Carl said. "Did you take the job? Did they interview you?"

"You didn't get my messages?"

"No. I … no …" Dawning realization crept into his voice. "I haven't been home in over a week. Jesus, Lyle, you took it, didn't you?"

"Well, yeah!"

"You've got to quit! You've got to quit now. Don't even go in tomorrow. Just call them, tell them you've changed your mind and you're finished."

"I can't do that, Carl! That's ridiculous!"

"If you don't quit, you'll—" The connection died in an abrupt flare of static.

Restore From Backup first published in 2007 by Bad Moon Books
Afterword first published 2007 by Bad Moon Books
"Algorithms of the Heart" first published 2016 in Clickers Forever by Thunderstorm Books
CoverDesign by David Dodd
ISBN 978-1-946025-68-5
For information address Crossroad Press at 141 Brayden Dr., Hertford, NC 27944
A Macabre Ink Production - Macabre Ink is an imprint of Crossroad Press.
www.crossroadpress.com

Crossroad Press Trade Edition

RESTORE FROM BACKUP

BY J. F. GONZALEZ & MIKE OLIVERI

ACKNOWLEDGMENTS

Mike Oliveri would like to thank Jesus for pushing this puppy through, Brian for pairing us up, Dave at Crossroad Press, Rich for the IT training (I am the master now), and Melissa for more than I could ever list here.

Both authors would like to thank Tom and Elizabeth Monteleone for pointing out what we knew all along.

J. F. Gonzalez would like to thank Mike, Brian, Cathy and Hannah, and all the IT guys and gals in various IT related jobs past and present for unknowingly providing much of the inspiration and background of this novella.

CONTENTS

CHAPTER ONE

One would think that a man who spent his days rescuing users from the perils of their desktop PCs would at least be adept at something like maintaining an email address book. Lyle Harrison, at least in this particular case, embodied the oxymoron "Luddite technician."

He dug up Carl Sanders's telephone number from the well-thumbed Rolodex he still maintained from his college days. Melissa teased him about it all the time, but he carried the Rolodex from job to job like a good luck charm. From professors and frat brothers to bars and pizza joints, the numbers and addresses were all in there. When he sought his first job following graduation, he flipped through the cards and stumbled on the number of a high school friend he hadn't heard from in years. On a whim, Lyle had given him a ring. One thing had led to another, and before Lyle knew it he'd landed a fat job at Anderson & Associates.

That lasted until two months ago. He'd survived the bulk of the cuts when the bottom fell out of the IT industry, but thanks to the recent trend to move technical jobs overseas to reduce labor costs, the layoff axe found the back of Lyle's neck. Another six months of this and he'd be able to tear the unemployment office's address out of his Rolodex; no sense calling them after they stop handing out checks.

The phone rang. Lyle lifted the cordless handset and glanced at the Caller ID display in time to see Melissa's cell number scroll across the screen. He thumbed the talk button. "Hello."

"Hi, babe," his wife responded in a worn voice.

"Are you still at the hospital?"

"Yeah, still in the pediatric wing, still waiting on test results."

"That figures," he replied evenly. Inside, he wanted to scream. He quickly changed the subject. "How's the little guy holding up?"

"Gabe's good. He's sleeping again. All this excitement has really worn him out. They gave him some more ice cream for lunch, though, so he's not complaining."

Lyle couldn't blame him. Three middle-of-the-night ER visits in five days would take their toll on anyone, especially a kid just creeping up on his first year. Last night had been especially bad, and while the doctors managed to get Gabriel's wheezing under control, they had to use a sedative to calm him down. It broke Lyle's heart to see his son like that, and it sure didn't help matters that his health benefits were long gone.

"Well that's good. Have you eaten?"

"The nurses brought me lunch with Gabe's. They're a lot better than the night shift. How about you? Having any luck?"

"I'm getting ready to call Carl."

"Carl? I thought you didn't want to pester him again?"

Lyle harrumphed. "I don't. I feel like a leech. But at this point, I don't feel we have much choice." As he spoke, his fingers found the card and fished it out. The blue pen had faded some but was still easily legible.

"I'm sure he'll understand."

"What did the school say when you called in sick?"

"They already had a sub lined up, just in case. They understand."

Maybe so, but her sick time was far from unlimited. Her salary and benefits carried them through, but without his health insurance to provide dual coverage, Gabe's medical bills would tax her meager income to its extreme. Lyle feared that even if he found a job, he'd be denied coverage based on his son's pre-existing condition—whatever *that* was.

"Well, I better let you go. I'm going to try to catch some sleep while Gabe's napping."

"Okay, hon. Do you want me to come down there?"

"No, that's okay. You do what you've gotta do. We'll be fine, and I'll call you as soon as I hear something."

"Alright, then. I love you."

"I love you, too." She clicked off the line and he set down the phone.

Gabriel's physician had ordered a spirometry and the usual battery of X-rays and blood tests. One would think at least some of those results had come back. At least cystic fibrosis had been ruled out (thank God). He didn't know if he would have been able to handle that one.

He glanced at the clock. Almost one o'clock. He thought about driving down to the hospital anyway, but he had Carl's work number in hand so he decided he may as well call. He just hoped Carl had fared better than he had in the IT slump.

Carl answered on the second ring. "Yeah?"

"Carl! How you doing? It's Lyle!"

"Hey, Lyle, how's it going?"

The instant recognition in Carl's voice steadied Lyle's nerves, and for the next ten minutes they talked as if they had seen each other only yesterday; in reality, it had been almost two years—not since Melissa got pregnant, if Lyle remembered correctly. The obligatory "how is everyone?" question came around, and Lyle tried to keep the worst of the doom and gloom out of it as he relayed his situation.

"What have you been up to?" Lyle asked.

"Same old shit, really. Sometimes I wonder why I got my degree in Computer Science in the first place, what with our jobs being handed to the dotheads."

"Yeah, I hear that," Lyle said, thinking *this is it, this is where you start your beg and pitch session.* "Speaking of which, one of those dotheads just got handed my job. I've been out of work for two months."

"Are you serious? Damn, that sucks! I'm sorry to hear that." The sincerity in his voice felt genuine, giving Lyle a pang of guilt.

"I can't find anything, man. Place I worked at moved the whole fucking IT division to India—programming, networking, help desk, software and web development, all of it. Shit, I think they would have laid off the technical writers if they knew they could find anyone fluent enough in English to write technical manuals."

"That's a shame," Carl said. "And it's all gonna bite us on the ass sooner or later."

"Yeah. Listen, if you hear about anything on your end, could you let me know? Keep me in mind?"

"Sure thing, man. Anything I could do to help, no problem. You still do web development?"

"Oh yeah. I thought about doing it full time, but since the suits took all the fun out of coding HTML it's not a great market to get into."

"You can say that again. Hey, you do any networking?"

"A little."

Carl paused. Lyle could almost hear the gears turning in his friend's skull. He pictured Carl at work, feet kicked up on his cluttered desk in some cramped cubicle somewhere in a Manhattan skyscraper, cell phone to his ear, fingers twirling a pen. "Listen, I may have something for ya. They're looking for network administrators—Unix and Windows Server. I know you're all big on Unix, but how are your Windows Server skills?"

"Pretty decent," Lyle said. He'd farted around with Windows Server enough at his last job to be Microsoft Certified, but no fucking way was he dropping fifteen grand into Bill Gates's pocket just for a little piece of paper with Microsoft's blessing to handle their product.

"I figured," Carl said. Lyle could hear him shuffling some papers around on his desk. "I mean the shit isn't exactly brain surgery, right?"

"Exactly!" Lyle laughed. Maybe he'd made the right decision after all.

"Alright, you're going to give Anita Martinez a call." Carl rattled off a phone number with a 976 area code. "She's our West Coast IT Division Manager. Tell her I told you to call her. I'm going to send her an e-mail right now, so she'll be expecting your call."

"Who do you work for?"

"Kaiser Development Systems."

"And you know for a fact they're hiring?"

"I see the job boards on our intranet. A new posting just went up this morning. Network Administrator, Unix and Windows Server, TCP/IP skills, IIS, yada yada yada, and all the other associated acronyms." They laughed. Last time they talked, Lyle bitched about how the IT industry—how the entire business world, it seemed— was being overrun by acronyms. Corporate and technical glossaries were filling entire volumes on their own.

"Really, I think you'd be a perfect fit," Carl continued. "I'm doing something similar and I'll tell you, it's a piece of cake. I'm getting sixty a year just watching the little network lights blink, you know?"

"Sixty?" Not wonderful in the Grand Scheme of All Things Technical, but still eight grand more than he'd made at Anderson.

"Yup. And the benefits are great, too. Full medical and dental, no deductible. They'll pay for shit other plans won't pay for, like chiropractic care, and they start you off with three weeks' vacation a year, they match your 401k contributions, and their pension plan is—"

"You don't have to tell me any more, I'm sold." Completely. Some of those bennies made the salary more than workable.

"Good. Now leave me the hell alone and call Anita."

Which he did. He pushed the off button to disconnect, then immediately hit the talk button and dialed the number Carl had given him.

"Good afternoon, Kaiser Development West. May I help you?"

"Yes, I'd like to speak to Anita Martinez, please."

"Who shall I say is calling?"

"Lyle Harrison."

"Thank you, Mr. Harrison. One moment."

On came the hold music. "The Girl from Ipanema" if he remembered right. He hummed along as he leaned back in his chair and stretched.

"Mr. Harrison," a woman said abruptly. He sat up and reached for a pen. "I was just now reading an email from Carl Sanders about you."

"Ah, perfect timing, then." He hoped. "He gave me your number."

"So I gathered."

He winced. He hoped this wasn't starting things on the wrong foot.

"So you're looking for a job," she said. "Tell me about yourself."

He did, keeping to an old professor's advice to toot his own horn. Carl had said she was an IT director, so he didn't bother to water down the tech stuff the way he would for a personnel department drone. She interjected once or twice, asking him to elaborate on specific projects he'd worked on, or to explain how he had resolved certain problems. They spoke for fifteen minutes, keeping it all business, and she closed by asking him to email a current résumé to her. He jotted down her address, they said goodbye, and he made sure the phone was hung up before letting out a grand sigh of relief.

He felt good about the call. For the first time in weeks, he felt optimistic. He decided to go down to the hospital anyway, and smiled most of the way there.

CHAPTER TWO

The next few weeks were so hectic and nerve wracking that Lyle thought he would be committed before all was said and done.

The hospital discharged Gabriel, but he still went through another battery of tests. He had another breathing attack, and while they sat with him in the hospital, their pediatrician called and said the results from the last tests came in and it was official—Gabriel was diagnosed with a mild case of asthma.

Lyle and Melissa took the news with great relief, but Lyle noticed Dr. Walker's puzzlement as he sat down with them in his office. Melissa held Gabriel, who batted at a toy she waved over his head. The joy and happiness pouring off of her was intoxicating, and if Dr. Walker's puzzled expression hadn't caught Lyle's eye, he would have been drunk with the same kind of joy. As it was, he turned to Dr. Walker curiously.

"Is everything okay?"

"Yes, everything's fine," Dr. Walker said. He flipped through Gabriel's file, that look of puzzlement still on his face; lips pursed, brow furrowed in concentration as he read the reports, searching for something. "It's just remarkable."

"What's that?" Lyle asked.

"Does Gabey like to have SpongeBob fly through the air and dive-bomb his face like *this*!" Melissa cooed in baby-talk voice. She made a mock dive with a plastic SpongeBob toy toward Gabe's face. He laughed hysterically.

"It's remarkable that whatever it was your son came in with three or four weeks ago has been downgraded to a simple case of asthma."

Lyle knew what Dr. Walker was getting at; he remembered

those early conversations with him and the other specialist he had brought in to examine his son. "You thought it was a rare strain of cystic fibrosis, but the first blood tests ruled that out."

"Yes, and it also ruled out asthma. As did the CT scans and X-rays."

Lyle glanced quickly at Melissa, who had just tuned in to the conversation. "For a while there we were both pretty scared," Lyle said. "The fact that you guys didn't know what it was—"

"Was it just a misdiagnosis?" Melissa asked. She propped Gabe into a sitting position on her knee and bounced him gently as he chewed on SpongeBob's head and drooled.

"Oh, no, not at all," Dr. Walker replied, banishing the very idea of somebody in his profession making such a mistake. "Asthma would have shown up on an X-ray. Very easy to spot. And allergies would have shown up in the blood work and nasal smears. The eosinophils count was normal and, if you remember, his first X-ray and CT scans were clear. He had all the symptoms though— wheezing, shortness of breath, rattling cough."

"Yeah, I remember," Lyle said.

"That's why I thought it was a respiratory infection," Dr. Walker said. "Sometimes respiratory infections are caused by a virus rather than bacteria, which is the primary cause of asthma, but our tests came back negative."

"Except for that last blood test," Melissa said.

"Right, and that's the one that has everybody in the lab talking." Dr. Walker leaned back, drumming his pen on the desk. "I'm sorry about that day, having to come back to Gabe to get another vial of blood."

"That's okay," Melissa said, holding Gabe. When the baby had seen the nurse coming at him with the syringe, he had started screaming. Hopefully it wouldn't be a lasting image for him or instill a permanent fear of doctors. His routine shots were bad enough.

"But you still saw the same thing," Lyle said.

"Yes. An abnormal red cell count and activity, oddly shaped white cells ... an abundance of them, which would indicate an infection of some sort. Nothing you would think to cause breathing problems resembling asthma, but we thought they were evidence of something else. That's the direction we were going in."

"Until last night when we brought him in again," Melissa said, trading glances with Lyle. Gabriel traded SpongeBob's head for his right fist.

"And last night's blood work showed all the signs pointing toward asthma, so we ordered another chest X-ray and presto! The evidence was right there!" He slapped the file, shaking his head. Lyle caught just the faintest notion that Dr. Walker was not embarrassed by the misdiagnosis, but baffled and disturbed. "We ran another blood test to check for the same white cell count that showed up last time and they were all gone. Not a trace. It was as if whatever it was had morphed or regressed to a simple case of asthma."

"How is that possible?" Lyle asked.

Dr. Walker sighed. "I don't know." He looked across his cluttered desk at Lyle and Melissa. He was a middle-aged man with wispy gray hair, wearing wire-framed glasses perched on a beak of a nose. His white lab coat was drawn over a white dress shirt and blue slacks, his name sewn on the right breast pocket of the coat. "I've never heard of any disease regressing to a lower form before. I don't even know what Gabe had before we made the asthma diagnosis. We were still trying to identify the variants in his blood work when you came in last night."

Dr. Walker's tone of voice, the seriousness of how he reacted to the latest developments in Gabriel's case, changed Lyle's outlook. He felt a spike of fear for his son worm its way into him, and he reached out and touched his little boy and tickled his tummy playfully. "Is this something we should be worried about?"

"In all honesty, I don't know. If you were to take Gabe to another physician they'd probably make the same diagnosis. Will his condition change? Based on his last test results, I doubt it. Once asthma is identified at this stage, antibiotic treatments help control it. I don't see it mutating into something worse now that we've caught it this early."

"But what about the other stuff you found?" Melissa asked, the worry creeping into her voice now.

"I don't know," Dr. Walker said, and now it looked to Lyle like maybe he was embarrassed. It was possible Gabe's blood work was mislabeled in the lab. He brought this up to Dr. Walker, who shrugged. "I doubt it, especially with the measures the government imposes. I think the best thing we can do is put Gabriel on the antibiotic regimen and monitor him. Get the prescription filled and let me see him next week. I'll want to run another series of tests—blood, CT and X-ray. In the meantime, I think we should count ourselves lucky."

Lyle left feeling more confused than he knew he should have, but when he saw the color in Gabriel's cheeks, saw the playfulness in his eyes, he knew that his son had passed some kind of milestone. Somehow, whatever it was that the doctors had been frantically tearing their hair out trying to diagnose last week had receded into a simple case of asthma.

It worried him, too, and the latest medical bills—hospitalization, tests, antibiotics—would take another chunk out of Melissa's income.

Anita Martinez called the afternoon of their visit with Dr. Walker, again all business. They arranged an interview the following week, and he used that time to bone up on a few Windows commands and administrative techniques, as well as line up two more interviews with other companies.

The Honda's yellow *Check Engine* light came on the next morning, a Tuesday, and when it failed to turn off by itself the following day, he took it to the garage and was informed that it would be a three-hundred-and-fifty-dollar job. Gabe's antibiotics ran out, producing another bill, plus groceries, mortgage, taking suits to be dry-cleaned, replacing the vacuum cleaner … the hits just kept on coming.

He fumbled his first interview for a web developer position at an advertising agency. He could tell halfway through it that he was over-selling his technical skills and not enough of his creative strengths, which was funny since he had started out at Anderson as a graphic artist before moving to the IT department. Later that week they brought Gabe in for his follow-up appointment, and on the morning Lyle left for his interview with Anita, they received the news that their son's condition had not changed: mild asthma. No weird things in the blood, give him these antibiotics, three hundred and fifty dollars, please.

The interview with Anita went well. He felt nervous through most of it, but either she didn't notice or didn't care. He eased into it, and thought he did rather well during the verbal portion. Sensing she was a no-bullshit type of manager, he decided to be honest with everything—no hyping his rather weak programming skills. If she asked, he'd tell her he had a little experience in those areas, period.

Fortunately, she never asked about his programming experience, so he didn't volunteer his shortcomings.

They talked about networking and all the protocols; they talked about security and firewalls. Anita asked Lyle to give her a rundown of his daily routine at his former job, which he did. She nodded, jotting down notes behind a large gray desk as he talked. She was a pleasant-looking woman, dressed impeccably in a gray business suit with her blonde hair pulled straight back. When he finished, she smiled and leaned forward.

"I'll be perfectly honest with you," she said, her voice crisp and business-like. "The position we're considering you for is an entry-level Systems Network Administrator position. I'm very impressed with your background, and I like the fact that you started out as a computer graphic artist and web master on the Unix side. I take it you were using Macs?"

Lyle nodded. "Oh yeah."

"We run a strict Unix shop here, but we also have a Windows Server network. I like that you have experience on both platforms. In the position you're applying for, you'd be dealing with both considerably."

This piqued Lyle's interest, and she took him on a quick tour through the facility. The place was very impressive. They owned the entire building, which resided in a large, corporate industrial park in Irvine. Lyle immediately noticed the marble flooring in the lobby, and brass accents marked every door and most of the walls. Whatever it was Kaiser Development Systems did, they pulled down a good buck doing it.

Anita filled him in a little more during the short tour. "KDS is the largest developer of software and network support for the international medical community. Our main corporate offices are in New York and Athens, and we have campuses on every continent but Antarctica, though we may change that this year with a science team we're looking to sponsor. Our division services the entire West Coast and Canada; our Chicago office services the Midwest, and New York services the East Coast."

She showed him the data center and Lyle noted the racks of

servers along one wall, along with various tape backup systems. A row of cubicles lined the opposite wall, all within the brightness of a white-tiled, climate-controlled computer room. It was amazing; the setup told Lyle they were huge, but he'd never heard of them before. "As you can see, we maintain state-of-the-art equipment," Anita said. "We also provide the best training. Should you be interested in strengthening your technical skills, we can arrange that, no problem."

Lyle came away from the interview feeling very positive, especially the way she kept saying "you could do this" and "you will do that."

He told Melissa all about it at length that evening.

"I hope you get it," she said. "It sounds like a wonderful opportunity. You think you'll like working there?" She spooned mashed carrots into Gabriel's mouth.

"I think so." Lyle leaned against the kitchen counter. "It's in Irvine … kind of a long drive, but the pay and the benefits sound great."

"I don't want to push you into it if you don't think you'll like it," Melissa said, wiping Gabriel's chin with a bib. "But we're going to need the money."

"I know." All thoughts of the job went out the window as Gabriel coughed suddenly and went into another mild asthma attack.

CHAPTER THREE

Lyle blinked in surprise when he read the words "Kaiser Development Systems, Inc." off the face of the Caller ID box a week later. The phone rang a third time, a fourth, as he gawked at it.

"Who is it?" Melissa asked as she spooned a mouthful of mashed peas into Gabriel's mouth.

"Kaiser Development," he muttered. A week of nothing. He was all set to write it off as a failure. Yet now the phone rang.

"Aren't you going to pick it up?" Her tone tagged the word "goofball" at the end of the sentence.

Lyle blinked. What if it wasn't to offer him a job? What if they just wanted to say "thanks, but no thanks, loser" and hang up on him? Maybe he should let the machine get it …

"Well?" Melissa paused from feeding Gabriel. She looked at him. He picked up the handset. "Hello?"

"May I speak to Lyle Harrison please?" a familiar voice asked.

"Speaking."

"Hi, Lyle, this is Anita Martinez at KDS."

"Hi, Anita. What can I do for you?"

"Well, my associates and I have had an opportunity to review your application and discuss our interview the other day, and we'd like to offer you the Systems Administrator position. Are you still interested?"

"Yes, absolutely!" He suppressed a whoop and shot a thumbs-up to Melissa. She gasped and jumped out of her chair. Gabriel burbled and shoved his fist through his mushed carrots.

"Great! Then let me be the first to say welcome aboard. I'm very pleased to have you as a member of our team. I think your technical background will be a tremendous asset."

"I hope so," Lyle said. "I'm looking forward to getting started."

"You'll love your cubicle, too," Anita said quickly. Lyle could tell by the background noise—shuffling paper, rustling of coats and briefcases—that she was preparing to leave for the day and was in a hurry. "You'll have three boxes set up in your cubicle—two PCs running Windows and Unix, and one Mac. It'll be just like your old job at Anderson."

"Sounds great!"

They spent a few moments affirming the salary and benefits they had discussed during his interview the previous week, and she asked him if he could start on Monday. He assured her that yes, he could, and that he would report to her at 8 a.m. sharp. She told him how to get through the security gate, reminded him of the dress code, and said goodbye.

He hung up and turned to his wife, who suddenly stood beside him. She grabbed the sides of his face and kissed him firmly, then hugged him.

"It's about time something good happened to you," she said. "I'm proud of you."

"I thought I'd never hear from them again!" he admitted, returning the hug. "Oh, this is great." He kissed her on the forehead.

"*Ba!*" Gabe shouted, followed by a string of jealous babble. Green and orange muck covered most of his face and hands.

"Okay, I'm coming," Melissa assured their son. She grabbed a washrag from the sink and sat down beside Gabe's highchair.

Lyle felt relieved that he would start work Monday. Despite the fact that his network administration skills were a bit rusty, he was positive he could do a good job. Thanks to California employment law, Kaiser could only verify that he'd held a similar IT position at Anderson, had no criminal record, and held a bachelor's degree from an accredited university. They had no reason to send spooks to ferret out personal and work-related information from his former co-workers; after all, it was just an IT position, not national security.

Except … something worked its way into the back of his mind. He thought about it, trying to keep his happy face on for Melissa so she wouldn't notice. She babbled excitedly about how they could finally get some bills paid off—maybe take that vacation to the Sierras they'd been talking about. Lyle nodded and kept up that smile.

"… Just like your old job at Anderson," Anita had said. The phrase wormed through his gut and wouldn't leave him alone. It was a little thing, really. He could've mentioned it in passing to her during the interview, but the more he thought about it, the more he was certain that he'd never once told her about his cubicle setup at Anderson. About how he'd juggled three computers on his desk—a Windows workstation, a Unix workstation, and a PowerMac.

Of course, he'd mentioned his dabbling in all three platforms in his design days, so maybe she decided to set his desk up in a similar fashion. Maybe she was one of those New Age managers consumed by effectiveness, figuring a reminder of his old job would help him ease into the new job, kind of like nurturing the geek homeostasis.

Then again, maybe she talked to somebody at Anderson. Maybe she said to hell with the law, and talked to one of his co-workers or his old supervisor. It could never officially appear on his application materials, but nothing stopped her from doing it.

No, that was impossible. The closest Kaiser's HR department could have gotten in verifying previous employment would have been Anderson's HR Department. There's no way Anita Martinez would have been able to get information out of any of his former co-workers or his old boss.

So how had she known about his setup at Anderson?

CHAPTER FOUR

The first two days on the job went by without much hassle. They dropped him in the department which served as the Help Desk Call Center for the company's U.S. branches, and did dual work maintaining the network servers and the private intranet and public Internet servers. The abundant orientation materials broke down the corporate infrastructure in greater detail than Anita even alluded to, and he learned that all major corporate IT decisions came out of this building. One of the stockholder books even had a rather attractive mug shot of Anita near the end.

As for his new home, the lower-level systems administrators all worked on the first floor. Once past the lobby and the security booth, employees walked down a corridor leading to the work areas and cafeteria. The servers Anita showed him during his interview were housed on this floor, complete with raised flooring, accessible only by a numeric keypad and radio frequency key fob. Five cubicles ran the length of the room and more server equipment resided in a similar room across the hall, the only difference being the backup tape library and robot which replaced two cubicle spaces on that side.

Lyle shared the second cubicle in the main room with his second- and third-shift counterparts. He only saw them for a few minutes at a time each day as he relieved the latter and was in turn relieved by the former. He got the distinct impression they were less than thrilled with him for landing a coveted first-shift position, but he didn't lose sleep over it as the two technicians he spent the bulk of his day with seemed like decent guys. Anita supervised them from her third-floor office and made frequent but unobtrusive visits to their cubicles. It made him nervous at times, but at least he could see her and get an idea of where she was coming from rather than guessing at cold, unfeeling decrees delivered via email.

Most of his job involved working with the software backups. Once the backup process completed, he would check and recheck them, verifying first that the data had transferred properly and that it would be readable off the media. The rest of the time they ran calculations against some mysterious binary files. They were some proprietary format he was unfamiliar with, and the in-house software would manipulate that data and spit out a series of cryptic results. Those results, in turn, were uploaded to a series of file servers and placed in the backup rotations.

The only thing nobody would tell him—not even the copious orientation manuals—is exactly what the company *did*, either generally speaking or with those data files. It further surprised him that given the size of the company and the number of people they employed worldwide, KDS never appeared in any of the standard trade magazines.

"So, what exactly do we do here?" he had asked Keith Jamison and Bob Hetfield at the end of his first week. Their cubicles were directly across from his, and they'd grown accustomed to chatting casually as Lyle slowly acclimated to his new routine.

"Does it matter?" Keith asked, not looking at Lyle as he tapped away on his keyboard.

Lyle frowned. "I don't know. I suppose not."

"Then do yourself a favor and forget it."

Keith had his back to him, so Lyle spun his chair around and peeked over the cubicle wall at Bob. Bob shook his head slowly and deliberately and looked away.

"Oohh-kay …" He turned back to his monitor and checked the progress of a backup job. His mail client chimed a few seconds later, notifying him of an email from Bob. It lacked a subject line. The body read "We'll talk later."

The soft thrum of his drumming fingers echoed in the kneehole of his desk. He clicked the reply button and positioned his fingers to respond, then thought better of it, closed the message and deleted it. Hard to say if someone monitored his mail queue.

He emailed Carl the following Monday to thank him for turning him on to the gig; he'd left Carl a voicemail the evening he got the job, but Carl never returned the call. Lyle assumed he had been busy, or perhaps out of town.

The rest of the week went great. Gabriel appeared to feel much better, and Melissa seemed happy and relieved that he enjoyed the job so far. She seemed especially interested in the benefits package he brought home, and spent one night reading through it while he played with Gabriel on the floor.

"You've got it good here, Hon," she said, flipping through the benefits papers he brought home to fill out. "Their medical benefits are wonderful! There's a five-dollar copay on everything, and their prescription drug plan is the best I've ever seen! And your choice of doctors … Wow, I can't even imagine the network they're tapped into."

"Oh yeah?" Lyle asked, eyebrows raised.

"Yeah. And a nice 401k and pension … you're not only vested at the five-year mark, they match your 401k contributions one hundred percent! That's unheard of!"

"No shit?" He found it hard to believe himself that the benefits at KDS were so great. "A hundred percent? Most companies don't contribute at all! Anderson sure as hell didn't."

"I know." Melissa flipped through the folder one more time. "This is just amazing. You really lucked out with this company. Really."

"I guess so." Lyle tickled Gabriel, who giggled and batted Lyle's fingers.

CHAPTER FIVE

As the first week passed, Bob never brought up his peculiar email. When Lyle pressed him in the cafeteria on Friday, Bob would only say KDS designed, maintained, and implemented various programming and software packages for the international medical community. It was the same drill he'd gotten from Anita during the interview process and from the orientation materials. Lyle finally decided Bob must have been screwing with him, and almost forgot about it.

Kevin went upstairs to speak with Anita about some work-related problem, and Bob took Lyle to the tape vault. The bulk of the extensive library was kept in the fireproof room, accessible only through a door around the corner from the servers. When the tapes reached the end of their rotation, the techs packed them for shipping to an off-site location for safekeeping as part of their Disaster Recovery Program. The DRP itself resided in a three-inch-thick red binder packed with dense pages and diagrams covering everything to do with the backup routine down to the most minute detail. Couriers arrived every morning to pick up the latest batch of tapes and to drop off older units to put back into rotation.

Bob referred to the DRP frequently, and told Lyle to read it thoroughly. He laughed, but Bob didn't.

"We're the backbone of everything," Bob said. He was a young guy, maybe twenty-eight, with short-cropped brown hair and thick glasses. He was originally from Texas and spoke with a slight twang, and he favored dark slacks and ties. "We maintain all the servers, make sure everything is running, monitor all network traffic, and we run the daily backup volume calculations …"

It was the same drill Lyle had heard several times in training.

They weren't getting it. He understood all that; what he wanted to know was, how did his department fit in with helping KDS achieve its overall goals?

Whatever *those* were.

He let Bob run through the routine one more time, and he nodded at all the right places. He asked several questions, picturing himself in some of the worst events possible, and Bob gave him the rundown on company protocol.

"The DRP is foolproof," he said. "It has to be. Now listen, I'm going to mention this to you today only because the last few alerts we got happened fairly recently, and Anita is going to explain the procedures for them to you after your probation period. Until then, when you get an e-mail or phone message from corporate regarding a Code Yellow, you come to me. Immediately."

Lyle raised an eyebrow. "What's a Code Yellow?" He didn't recall any color codes coming up during training. Maybe he had better take a closer look at the DRP after all.

"A network security warning. We run a tight ship here, but occasionally bugs get past our network. I'm not talking about normal viruses either. A Code Yellow is a step above that, and usually we're the first to hear about it, but occasionally the New York office picks up on it first. They'll issue the warning, then we go into action. It's no big deal, really. They're actually pretty rare."

"Hmm. Good thing."

When Bob finished his spiel, he returned to his desk and checked the three monitors placed strategically around his desk. He watched traffic on three different platforms, from three different parts of the country, and he had no idea why KDS even bothered to work on three different platforms. He figured they would be like most large corporations and be consistent throughout—either straight UNIX or straight Windows Server. Instead, they juggled the various platforms and operating systems and even seemed to have redundant data across all three of them.

He felt he could do his job better if someone would just explain the reasoning to him, but if everybody wanted to be so goddamn vague about it, then fine. He'd punch in, do what they paid him to do, and punch out. Lyle sat back in his chair and clicked over to the Unix screen to check the progress of a tape backup. Only a few more hours until quitting time.

He wondered if anyone would notice if he installed a copy of NetHack on the Unix box.

CHAPTER SIX

That evening after work, Lyle held Gabriel in his lap and watched CNN while Melissa cooked supper. She rattled off her day's encounters with aging coworkers as he made obligatory remarks that he hoped would give her the illusion that he was listening. He was more interested in the news, especially the report on the resurgence of the SARS outbreak.

"… and you wouldn't believe it," Melissa said as he heard her dump a can of tomato sauce in a pot. "Those old bats at the school are the most crankiest, orneriest old biddies you've ever seen, and—"

"Really?" Lyle bounced Gabriel on his knee. On TV the anchor reported the grim facts: thought to have been contained last year, SARS suddenly came back with a vengeance in New York. Eighteen people were admitted to area hospitals. The Centers for Disease Control weren't calling it a return of the epidemic yet, but they were concerned. Scientists flocked in from all around the world and already the first reports of similar cases had rolled in from Philadelphia and Toronto.

"Hey, honey, did you hear anything about this SARS thing?" he called.

"What?" Melissa asked, obviously annoyed that he had derailed her train of thought.

"SARS. It's come back."

"Great! Just what we need!"

Lyle's cell phone rang. He scooped it out of his pocket and answered the call. "Hello."

"Lyle?"

At first Lyle couldn't recognize the voice. "Yeah?"

"It's Carl."

"Oh, hey! How you doing?" Lyle settled back on the sofa, cradling Gabe with his left hand as he held the phone to his ear with his right. "I'm glad you called. Listen, did you get my—"

"Are you at home?" His voice sounded urgent, almost panicked. He breathed heavily into the phone as he waited for Lyle's response.

"Yeah, I am. Why?"

"Okay … okay …" Lyle could hear the din of traffic between breaths. Judging by the proximity of some of the horns, it sounded like Carl was in the middle of Times Square.

"Carl, are you okay?" He hoped Carl hadn't been nailed with SARS. Or his family or something.

"No, I'm not buddy. I'm not okay. I'm in Chicago. It's the farthest I could get in this short of time, but I've got to make tracks and get the hell out of Chicago, too."

"What?" Lyle straightened up, his composure grave now. He lifted Gabriel out of his lap and gently placed him in a sitting position on the sofa next to him. Gabe laughed and flapped his arms. "Chicago? What are you doing there?"

"It was the first bus trip out of New York I could get. I had to get the fuck out, Lyle. You wouldn't believe what happened. Jesus Christ!" He sounded deathly afraid.

"Carl, what's up? Where are you, really?"

"I shouldn't have fucking said that. Jesus *fuck*, I'm stupid!"

"What are you talking about?"

"I've got to get out of here. I can't stay here, not after I've fucked up like this. *Fuck!*"

"Can't stay where? If you need help, you know I'm more than happy to do what I can for you. Hell, I owe you one and then some!"

"I can't tell you. I can't tell anybody. I have to be in hiding, okay? Nobody can find me."

"Why can't anybody find you?" He glanced up quickly to see Melissa standing in the living room doorway, looking concerned. He nodded and waved her back to the kitchen. *Everything's okay.* She frowned, her look saying, *Bullshit! You're telling me what's going on when you get off the phone.*

"The job!" Carl said. "Did you take the job? Did they interview you?"

"You didn't get my messages?"

"No. I … no …" Dawning realization crept into his voice. "I haven't been home in over a week. Jesus, Lyle, you *took* it, didn't you?"

"Well, yeah!"

"You've got to quit! You've got to quit *now*. Don't even go in tomorrow. Just call them, tell them you've changed your mind and you're finished."

"I can't do that, Carl! That's ridiculous!"

"If you don't quit, you'll—" The connection died in an abrupt flare of static.

Lyle jumped at the noise. He looked at the phone and pushed the Send button. The static came through stronger. Behind him, in the kitchen, Melissa asked, "What's going on?"

Lyle turned the phone off, momentarily confused and scared. Melissa approached him.

"Who was it, honey? Is everything okay?"

"Everything's fine," Lyle said, turning the phone back on. "I just got disconnected."

"Who was it?"

"Carl."

"Is he alright?"

"Yeah, I think so." Lyle went through his menu options to see if he could trace the number the call had originated from. "He just quit his job, though, and he sounded upset."

"Oh. I hope he's okay," she said, returning to the kitchen.

"I think he is," Lyle said. He found the number and dialed it. "He just sounded upset."

He placed the phone to his ear and listened as the phone rang half a dozen times. He was about to hang up when somebody picked up the receiver.

"Hello?" It sounded like a kid, maybe a teenager.

"Uh, hello? I'm trying to reach Carl?"

"Carl? Anybody around here named Carl?"

Lyle's stomach turned. He could hear background noises. Traffic, people talking, horns blaring.

The kid came back on the line. "Nobody here named Carl, man."

"Is this a phone booth I called?"

"Yeah."

"You see a guy at this phone booth a minute ago who was balding, kinda stocky, maybe wearing a goatee?"

"I don't think so, bro. I just got here."

"What city did I call?"

The kid laughed. "Chicago, man!"

The dread settled in the pit of Lyle's stomach as he punched the hang-up button. He found Carl's cell phone number in his address book and hit speed dial. The phone rang three times before a recorded voice came on the line: "The number you have reached is no longer in service. Please check the number and try your call again."

Damn! Lyle set the phone down, his heart racing.

What the fuck was going on?

Gabriel hopped up and down on the cushion. He rolled onto his back and came perilously close to the edge of the sofa. Lyle set him on the floor and the baby immediately flipped over on his stomach and began to crawl toward the television. Lyle sat forward, elbows on his knees, processing the telephone conversation.

Carl quit his job, left New York, apparently hiding from something. Just how long ago all this had happened, Lyle had no idea. He guessed maybe close to two weeks now. It had to have been at least that long. Carl had sounded surprised to hear the news that Lyle got the job at KDS, despite the voice and email messages.

How long has he been like this? When does a guy like Carl just up and leave a job?

It had to have been around the time he got hired. It would have taken a few days to get to Chicago by bus, which meant Carl had been wandering around the city for over a week.

Hiding out.

But why? And why beg Lyle to quit after setting him up with the job in the first place?

Something wasn't right. Carl had never been the most pragmatic person. He'd dabbled in methamphetamines back in school, which used to make him paranoid. Maybe Carl had slipped back into snorting speed and had hallucinated some grand plot against him. The last time this happened, Carl had been convinced that an army of government agents—the fabled Men in Black—were spying on him. They'd follow Carl all over Manhattan on the subways, and every time Carl tried to get off, a pair of them would be waiting at the top of the stairs leading to the city streets above, forcing him to descend back into the subway and catch another train to a random stop. But they'd never let him off. He claimed they kept him bouncing around New York all night until they finally let him out at 6 a.m. in Brooklyn to buy cigarettes.

"Did you try calling Carl again?" Melissa asked as she set out plates of spaghetti and marinara sauce on the table. Lyle set Gabe in his high chair while Melissa retrieved the garlic bread from the oven.

"I left a message on his voice mail. He'll call back."

Melissa let it go, and as much as Lyle tried to enjoy the rest of his evening he couldn't stop thinking about Carl.

CHAPTER SEVEN

Lyle glanced over his shoulder to make sure nobody paid any attention to him before opening up his email client. He'd thought about Carl's phone call all weekend and was actually glad to come into work the following Monday so he could investigate this further. He typed Carl's last name in the address field, then waited a few seconds while the program scanned the corporate directory for a match. It quickly returned a few options, but none of them Carl.

He did another quick search and found the name of Carl's supervisor in New York. He wrote the man a brief e-mail inquiring about Carl, claiming Carl had been helping him out on a project and wanted to confirm whether or not Carl was still with the company.

Thirty minutes later he got a response: *Carl resigned his position with KDS approximately two weeks ago.* The man offered no further explanation, and phone calls to Carl's apartment in Brooklyn went straight to voice mail. He left another message, though he didn't think it would do any good.

Lyle tried calling Carl's mom in Phoenix when he got home. He'd spoken to her perhaps half a dozen times in the eight years he'd known Carl, and she sounded worried.

"He called us once," she said. "He said he couldn't explain, that he was leaving his job and leaving New York. If you ask me, I'm afraid he's back on the drugs again. He sounded so paranoid."

He's tweaking, Lyle thought as he watched the news in the living room. The anchors spit out the same litany of crap: more U.S. soldiers killed by a suicide bomber in Iraq; Green River Killer Gary Ridgway admitted to an additional one hundred murders from Vancouver to San Diego in addition to the forty-eight he had originally confessed to; despite the sudden outbreak of what appeared to be a second wave of the SARS outbreak, it was quickly being contained with no new cases reported; the presidential candidates duked it out like a couple of heavyweight fighters; a new computer virus was wreaking havoc across computer networks in Europe and was expected to hit the U.S. tomorrow. He turned the TV off in disgust. With all the shit going on in the world, it was no wonder Carl freaked out.

The following morning Lyle read the corporate bulletin about the computer virus and spent the bulk of the day applying patches to the network systems. Applying and testing hot fixes easily ranked among the most tedious of computing duties, but it had to be done. Otherwise the complete opposite would occur; he'd be frantically attempting to clean out the virus, preventing its spread, and restoring lost systems from valid backups. Better bored than stressed to the eyeballs.

Melissa and Gabe arrived home shortly after he did, and he spent the rest of the evening with his family. He played with Gabriel, read fifty pages of the latest Stephen King novel, and that evening he and Melissa made love for the first time in a month.

It all helped keep his mind off things, but when he finally drifted to sleep his last thought was a hope that Carl was alright.

CHAPTER EIGHT

L yle received a curt summons to Anita's office at 10 a.m. the next morning.

"She needs me right now?" he asked the harried office attendant.

"That's what she said," the man replied, and quickly ducked back out of the server room.

"Great." He wondered what this was about as he double-checked the progress meter on the data verify job from last night's backup. Satisfied it wouldn't need his interaction for a little while, he headed for the elevator.

The clutter in her office took him by surprise. Stacks of paper and computer printouts covered her desk and the credenza behind her, and still more paperwork and binders jammed the bookshelves and spilled onto the floor.

"Close the door and have a seat," Anita said, motioning to one of the two chairs in front of her desk. A box of file folders and paperwork occupied the other. "Excuse the mess, I'm working on a big project right now."

Lyle closed the door and slid into the empty chair, praying none of this had anything to do with him. Anita picked up a stack of papers, riffled through them quickly, then placed them atop her filing cabinet. Dark circles lined her bleary eyes, and several strands of hair had escaped from her barrettes and stood out at odd angles. Her dark suit jacket lay across the credenza and its paperwork, and she had rolled the sleeves of her white blouse high on her arms and had opened the two top buttons.

"I just wanted to touch base with you and see how your first few weeks have been," she said. "How do you feel things are going?"

Lyle swallowed. "Things are going fine. I'm learning a lot. Bob and Keith have been wonderful showing me the ropes."

"So, they're getting you used to the routine?"

"Oh yeah." Lyle spent the next ten minutes or so detailing the various projects he was involved in: tape backup rotation, intranet search engine and file sharing and, of course, running the calculation binaries and uploading the results to the FTP server. "I'm still trying to figure out what that whole deal is. Keith said I'd just be more confused if he tried explaining to me what it was about, and that I'd be better off learning the job first and getting it down and worry about the rest later."

"That's probably a good idea."

"You think so?"

"Absolutely." Anita sat back in her black executive chair and regarded him calmly across the desk. "What we do at KDS is so complex that you have to approach it the way you would a huge jigsaw: one piece at a time. The more you learn, the more the pieces begin to fit together, and before long you begin to see a picture. And the more you learn your job and the systems, the more you learn the various jobs that contribute to the overall goal of KDS and then it becomes clearer.

"Trust me, I know what I'm talking about. When I first came to KDS, I didn't have a clue what we did despite all the buzzwords and having the corporate mission statement rammed down my throat in orientation. Mission statements usually mask the real purpose of a company's existence anyway, so I wouldn't even try guessing at the big picture just yet. You'll learn it eventually. What's important now is doing your job to the best of your ability and to be a team player. When you do that, the pieces will start falling into place. Does that make sense?"

"Yeah, I'm with you." *Maybe.*

"How's everything else going? Have you turned in your benefits paperwork?"

"Oh, yeah. Got that sent in early this week."

"Good. What about the workplace? Finding everything okay?"

Lyle shrugged. "Sure. I'm getting to know more and more people and I'm settling in. So far, so good."

"I'm glad to hear it." Anita leaned forward. Despite her exhaustion, she maintained her classy looks. A soft smile warmed her features. "You're doing great, Lyle, and I think you'll continue to do great things at KDS. We only select the brightest talent, and we're *very* picky."

Maybe that explained why he never saw any of their ads in the paper. They wouldn't be the first company who secured employees through specialized recruiters. "I'm just glad my friend Carl tipped me off. He used to work in the New York office."

"I hear he left the company. What a shame."

"Yeah, it surprised me, too. He really talked the place up before I applied."

"I take it you've spoken to him?" Her demeanor changed, albeit only slightly. Her brow angled slightly down, and her eyes turned flinty.

"Briefly." He felt reluctant to discuss specifics, and wondered if he had said too much already. "He just called to tell me he had resigned."

She stared him in the eye for a moment, just enough to make him squirm slightly. She then broke it off and sat back in her chair. "Well, I hope everything turns out okay with him. I understand he was an asset to our East Coast Division. Losing him was unfortunate."

Lyle didn't know what to say to that. Carl's words echoed to the forefront of his mind: *You've got to quit!*

"Well, enough of that," Anita said. "It's extremely rare to have employees just up and leave like that, so it takes me by surprise sometimes. Especially when it's someone of Carl's tenure. We pride ourselves on a high employee retention rate, which is why we offer such a generous benefits and compensation package. We want our employees to feel safe working for KDS and we want to earn their loyalty, not demand it."

"Well, I plan to stay as long as I can and to do the best job I can."

"Of course you do," Anita said. She stood up and Lyle did the same. She gently took his arm and walked him to the door. "We'll chat again in a couple of weeks, okay?"

"Okay."

"And if you have any problems don't hesitate to call me."

"I won't."

"Any questions?"

"No, ma'am."

"Good." She shook his hand. "If I don't see you tomorrow, have a good weekend. Enjoy that new Stephen King novel."

"I will," Lyle said. Anita smiled and waved goodbye as he exited her office and strode down the hallway to the elevators.

Wait a minute ... How did she know he was reading a King novel? He turned that over in his mind as he rode the elevator down to the first floor and returned to his cube. He tried to remember if he had brought the book to work, but was certain he hadn't. Normally he preferred to read the newspaper at lunch.

So how had she known he was reading the latest Stephen King novel?

The same way she knew you had a Mac, a Unix machine, and a PC on your desk at your old job, he thought. *Somehow she just ... knew.*

Lyle shivered; the data center seemed unnaturally quiet. He peered around his cubicle wall and saw Bob hunched over his keyboard, typing madly at his computer. He looked in the other direction and saw Keith leaning back in his chair, copying files to the server. They didn't seem bothered by anything.

"Hey, Keith," Lyle said, moving his mouse around the screen, not really having anything to say but wanting to break the silence anyway.

"Yeah?" Keith sounded bored.

"What're you doing this weekend?"

"Not much. Maybe go to the movies. You?"

"Oh, I don't know. Probably some reading."

"What are you reading?"

A peculiar thought struck him. "I'm finishing King's latest tonight, so I'll probably start into one of the Clive Barker books I haven't read yet this weekend."

"Isn't he the guy that writes books that are big enough to be doorstops?"

"Yeah, that's him."

They bantered casually for a few minutes until the conversation died, falling apart like a train derailing. Lyle looked at his computer screen, ignoring for the moment the jobs stacking up in his queue. He'd get to them; he could do that part of his job with his eyes closed. Instead he poked around at the latest calc binaries.

As usual, they revealed almost nothing beyond those cryptic

alphanumeric strings sprinkled with the occasional odd ASCII character. He glanced at the lengthening queue and sighed. Might as well get started.

He spent the rest of the day catching up and thinking about Anita. If she mentioned the Barker novel, he'd at least have a good idea how she got her information.

CHAPTER NINE

"You're on the Internet again?" Melissa asked. She used the tone reserved for those times he didn't pay enough attention to her.

He sat at the computer in their cramped study, guilty as charged. Gabriel slept soundly in his room. Melissa had been watching some chick flick on cable, which she'd wanted him to watch with her. He declined, citing a lack of desire to see Meg Ryan in yet another romantic comedy, and started digging for more information on Kaiser. Like before, he turned up little but their website and press clippings from a few tech organizations. Even the newsgroups turned up little to nothing. No smoking guns.

"I'm almost done," Lyle said. He returned to Google and considered how to word his next search.

"You're missing a good movie. I think you'll like this one; it's not as sappy."

"Okay, I'll be there in a minute." He took her assessment with a grain of salt. Anything starring Meg Ryan and Tom Hanks was a good movie in Melissa's eyes. She returned to the living room.

Lyle tapped a search term into the search line: software support for international medical community AND "kaiser development systems." He clicked Search. Google did its thing and returned the same results his last dozen inquiries had. He thought for a moment. He'd exhausted just about every way he could to search for information on the company, but what about his day-to-day activities?

He typed "binary files to aid medical research." Google returned a series of websites that had to do with math, binary files in general, distributed processing projects, medicine, pharmaceutical companies, and healthcare organizations. A couple pages in he decided he had just reached another dead end.

He clicked *File* on the browser menu and dragged the mouse down toward the Exit option. Before he clicked, a warning from his firewall popped up on the screen.

Description: Packet sent from 10.52.1.2 (UDP Port 2743) to 193.168.0.2 (UDP Port 68) was blocked.

Direction: Incoming

Date/Time: 2004/04/11

Type: Unknown

Lyle frowned as he considered the information. Though the average user rarely thought about it, hundreds—even thousands—of information packets came and went from their computer every second they spent online, zinging back and forth from the user's PC to the destination system, along countless routers and other systems and across the infinite paths available on the Internet. However, some of that traffic had no business on the average user's system, usually because it was irrelevant and sometimes because it was malicious.

Thus the firewall to block this unwanted traffic. By default, the firewall alerted him every time it blocked something. Because he didn't need to worry about each and every one of them, and because the alerts came fast and heavy when virus activity kicked up, he'd reconfigured the firewall to only throw out the flag for certain conditions.

This alert definitely fit into those criteria. For one, while his firewall recognized the intrusion attempt as a threat, it couldn't identify it. He'd never seen that before, and he updated his firewall and virus protection every few days to get the latest pattern files. And two, he recognized both IP addresses. The latter was simply the current IP address obtained from his service provider.

The second one, though, belonged to one of the main servers at KDS. He saw it every day. He supposed someone could be spoofing the address, a common tactic of hackers to prevent tracing them. But for them to be using a KDS address to attempt an intrusion on his network would be a big coincidence. What could a KDS system want with his home computer?

He could only come up with one conclusion. He tried to tell himself he was just being paranoid, but given the way things had been going lately, that one conclusion was the only one that made sense.

Somebody at KDS was trying to spy on him.

CHAPTER TEN

L yle stood on the raised floor in the control room, reviewing the audit log of the server that tried to get into his PC last night. He thought a quick search for his IP address would turn it right up, but that didn't work. Instead he reviewed the files manually, scanning the time period the alarm had gone off.

Bob approached him from behind and glanced over his shoulder. He sipped noisily from a cup of coffee. "How's the web server doing?"

"Lookin' good," Lyle said. He frowned in irritation. If he didn't hurry, Keith would transfer the evening's logs to another system for storage and purge the directory. "I was just checking to see if it was acting funny last night."

"Oh yeah? How come?"

"Something weird happened to my home PC." He quickly explained the warning his firewall had thrown up and the IP address it had flagged.

"That is weird," Bob confirmed. He took another hearty sip of coffee. "But it's probably nothing. If you were surfing the KDS site last night, this server might have flagged you. It's set up to do that in certain instances."

"Really?" He'd never heard of such a thing. While a good Intrusion Detection System could certainly be configured to do so, he didn't see much point in it. The website, after all, carried only public information. "Why?"

Bob shrugged. "Hell if I know. I just work here." Bob stepped off the raised platform and headed back to his cube.

Lyle turned back to the server. Okay, say it was configured to do that, and say that's exactly what it did. Why wasn't it in the logs?

Surely it reported those events somewhere. Perhaps it sent those logfiles to another system? That would make it more secure, so if the web server were ever compromised, the hacker wouldn't be able to tamper with the paper trail.

Damn. Lyle closed the terminal connection and slid the keyboard tray back into the rack, then headed back to his cube. He should have known the security boys would be well ahead of him; after all, their entire job was staying one step ahead of the hacker community.

A few minutes later, Bob got up and returned to the same terminal. He tapped away at the keyboard for a few minutes, then reviewed something on the screen.

"Hey, Keith?" Bob called. "You got a second?"

Lyle frowned as Keith got up and strode across the room. The two of them conversed quietly, and Keith crossed his arms. They both looked over at Lyle for a moment, then turned to the monitor and spoke some more. Finally, Bob nodded, typed on the keyboard for a moment, and closed up the terminal. They walked back to their cubicles together.

"Something wrong, guys?" Lyle asked.

"Nah," Keith said cheerfully. "Everything's cool."

"Then what was that all about?"

"One of the backup processes jammed up, that's all."

"Then why the staring?"

Keith scowled. "Hey, relax, man. It was one of your backup processes, that's all. We just didn't want to make a big deal out of it. Okay?"

Lyle felt his cheeks flush. "Oh. Sorry."

Bob harrumphed and shook his head, and then the two of them returned to their tasks.

Lyle feared maybe he was letting this whole business with Carl get to him. He had to work with these guys every day, too. It wouldn't be wise to piss them off.

However, when Lyle tried to access the web server later that afternoon, he got an access denied message. He retyped his username and password and received the same result. Against protocol, he tried to log in as the administrator directly. Again, access denied. He frowned, made sure the caps lock key was not on, and typed the password slowly and deliberately.

Access denied. The only explanation was that Keith or Bob had changed the password.

Lyle tried not to react, but anger welled up inside him. Maybe it was another coincidence. Or maybe he had broken some protocol he didn't know about. He doubted it, however; if it were that simple, Bob or Keith should have told him about it.

He packed up his stuff a few minutes before the end of his shift, and the moment the clock hit five he grabbed it all and left. He didn't say a word to Bob or Keith. Maybe he'd talk to them about things tomorrow when he felt calmer. For now, he decided he best just get out of there.

He stewed the whole way home, twice taking things out on other drivers. Melissa would have yelled at him for it if she'd been present, but fortunately she wasn't. Best vent it all now rather than unloading on her and Gabe, anyway.

Surprisingly, Melissa's car wasn't in the driveway when he arrived home. He grabbed his case, threw his blazer over his other arm, and nudged the door closed with his hip.

His cell phone rang.

"Dammit!" He set his case on the hood and threw his blazer over it, then pulled his cell phone off its clip on his belt. He thumbed the Send button before it could ring through to voice mail. "Hello?"

"Lyle, it's Carl."

"Carl?" Lyle glanced up and down the block, then grabbed his case and coat and headed for the house. "What's going on, man? What happened to you last week when you called?"

"Listen, I don't have much time. Have you quit your job yet?"

"No, I haven't quit! Will you tell me what the hell is going on?" Lyle dug into his slacks for his keys as he cradled the cell phone to his ear with his other hand. "You've really got me freaked out, Carl. Ever since you called I've been imagining my co-workers and my boss are spying on me."

"That's because they are."

Lyle turned the key and froze. "Say what?"

"Are you at home or in the car?"

"I just got home. I'm just about to go in the house."

"Don't go inside! I guarantee you the place is bugged."

Lyle's knees went weak and he felt nauseous. "Okay, cut the

bullshit, Carl. What happened? Where are you?"

"I'm somewhere safe. I can't tell you where … just in case. But I'm safe."

Carl didn't sound as frightened and paranoid as he had last time, but that gave Lyle little comfort. If Carl were back on the drugs, it would make all this a lot easier to accept. Lyle took a deep breath and stepped away from the front door. He tossed his case and coat on the porch bench.

"Listen, Carl … I need you to be straight with me, man. Hardly anyone outside the company has ever heard of KDS, and nobody on the inside will tell me what the fuck we do. One week you tell me it's a wonderful place to work, the next you're telling me to quit and you disappear. Please, tell me, what exactly is going on here?"

"KDS plants bugs in all new employees' homes to monitor their activities," Carl said.

"But *why*, God damn it? That's the part nobody will tell me!"

"I wish I could tell you more, Lyle, but it would take hours and I don't have that kind of time. We shouldn't even be talking about this over the phone. You don't deserve all this cloak and dagger bullshit. Please, just take my word for it and quit. Get yourself out of there now, and we'll get together another time."

"Jesus, Carl, I can't just fucking quit my job! I have a mortgage, a child—we're buried in debt from just trying to eat during the two months I was unemployed, and there's no telling what'll happen with Gabe's healthcare."

"There's more at stake here than just your house and your family, Lyle. The entire world is at stake here."

Lyle couldn't help but smile, but it was not one of humor. "Are you sure you're not back to snorting speed? Because it sure sounds like you're hallucinating something awful."

"Let me guess what you do all day," Carl said, ignoring his comment. "In addition to the usual humdrum systems administration, you spend the majority of your day running number-crunching schemes and posting the output to a remote site. Right?"

"Yeah, and?"

"You think you're the only one that does that?"

"I wouldn't think so."

"Who else?"

"Shit, I don't know. Probably the other two guys I work with, Bob and Keith."

"Would you be surprised if I told you *everybody* at KDS performs this job function?"

Lyle paused in mid-stride as he paced the porch. "That can't be right."

"It's true. Everybody from the CEO to the secretaries has a hand in them. Every spare cycle of every CPU in the entire company is devoted to processing those files, servers and desktops alike. They're done all around the world, every day, billions upon billions of calculations. It's performed at every level, on every computer."

"I don't understand," Lyle said.

"I don't have much time. I have a list of books I want you to get as soon as you can, even if you have to borrow them from the library. *The Golden Bough* by James Frazier, *Understanding the Kabbalah* by David Ellison, and *Footprints of the Gods* by James Nichols are the easiest to find. It might be tougher and more pricey if you can find a rare book dealer who has one, but you'll also need to find a copy of *Liber Daemonorum*—by Protassus. The Nichols book describes some of the theories that it's rumored to chronicle, but you're better off with the real thing."

Melissa's car appeared down the street. Lyle's heart was racing and his brain tried frantically to keep up. "That sounds like voodoo or something. What do they have to do with—"

"Shut up and listen!" Carl snapped. "Get to a bookstore tonight and at least pick up *Understanding the Kabbalah* and *The Golden Bough*. Read *The Golden Bough* first—the Kabbalah book will make a lot more sense if you at least get some background. I'll call you tomorrow."

Melissa pulled into the driveway. Lyle waved and turned away from her. "Listen, Melissa just got home. I gotta go."

"Promise me you'll find these books!"

"Yeah, I promise." He repeated the titles to himself to commit them to memory.

"Good. I'll call you tomorrow." Carl hung up.

Lyle shook his head as he returned the phone to his belt clip. He wondered who was more insane: Carl and his theories, or himself for believing them.

Melissa stepped out of the car. "Hey, honey, how you doing?"

"Fine. I just got home." Lyle forced himself to smile as he went to the car and gave her a kiss. His smile became genuine when he went to free Gabe from the car seat and the boy cried, *"Daa-eeee!"*

"Hey, buddy! Welcome home!" Lyle picked up his son and carried him toward the house. He stopped at the porch steps.

"Something wrong?" Melissa asked.

He frowned, thinking about the possibility of bugs listening to his every word. "Nah. What are we doing for dinner tonight? I'm starving."

CHAPTER ELEVEN

After supper, Lyle told Melissa he wanted to drop by the Barnes & Noble store at Metro Point to pick up a few books. Melissa nodded as she and Gabriel sat on the living room floor, playing with blocks.

"Pick me up a magazine?"

"Sure. What kind?"

"I don't care. *People* or *Entertainment Weekly* or something."

"Okay." Lyle put on his jacket and headed out.

When he arrived at the store he went straight to the Religion and Philosophy sections. He found *The Golden Bough* immediately and examined the cover copy. It didn't look all that interesting to him, as it appeared to be a history of superstition and religion from an anthropological point of view.

Understanding the Kabbalah lay buried among a number of books on Judaism and Jewish studies. It didn't look much better than *The Golden Bough,* and flipping through a few pages confirmed it. He shrugged and stopped by the magazine section to grab a copy of *Entertainment Weekly,* then checked out and went home.

When he arrived, he found Gabriel asleep in his bouncy seat. Lyle suspected the boy's bones must be made of rubber given the way he sat slumped to one side over the plastic tray and side rail.

"Hi, hon," Melissa greeted him. She sat snuggled up on her end of the sofa, the TV turned to some home improvement channel.

He leaned over and kissed her. "Hey, babe. Got your magazine." He pulled it out of the bag and handed it to her, and she thanked him as she spread it out on her lap. Lyle plopped himself down on his end of the sofa and dumped the bag on the center cushion. He considered the two books, then picked up *The Golden Bough* and wondered where to start.

It was 8 p.m. On the television, Bob Vila explained how easy it was to renovate a Victorian home in New England. Melissa went back and forth from watching *This Old House* and reading the latest celebrity poop. Lyle flipped through *The Golden Bough* for a bit, then picked up the Ellison book and flipped through it. He wondered what the hell these books on ancient magic and superstition had to do with KDS and their goals.

He tried to stay focused, though, and before long the book caught his interest. He hadn't seen a lot of this stuff before, and it was a nice break from technical manuals and HOW TO documents. When Melissa put Gabriel to bed and turned in herself, he chose to stay on the couch and read a bit longer.

CHAPTER TWELVE

Lyle clicked "OK" on a small dialog box and a plain red status bar in a blank gray window appeared in the center of his computer screen. A green sliver appeared on the left, and plain black text beneath the sliver metered out 1%. He dragged the box to the upper right corner of his screen, then leaned back and stretched. His spine crackled.

He'd woken up groggy that morning, yet eager to go to work after reading a section of *The Golden Bough*. He still had no idea what Carl was getting at, but perhaps if he paid closer attention to what he did today, and made careful observations regarding his daily tasks, he would begin to make the connections.

The puzzle would become clearer as the shapes fell into place. Isn't that what Anita had said last week?

The binary file calculations, for example. How many of them had he performed the last three weeks? A hundred? A thousand? He'd lost count after the first couple days, and he still had no clue what they were calculating. All he knew was he pointed a program at the next file in a queue that replenished periodically. Sometimes the calculations took a few minutes, others took over an hour. When they finished, the file went into another queue that someone else processed. Between calculations he made sure the backups ran, the network links were all up, and the servers handled the load.

He poked and prodded at one of the files around ten thirty, throwing everything at it from simple text editors to database queries. For the most part, the system simply denied him access.

Despite Bob's initial eagerness two weeks ago to explain what purpose their department served in the whole of the company, he quickly changed the subject every time Lyle tried to talk about the files. Even when they were alone, Bob would suddenly get nervous and evasive, then make an excuse to get away.

Lyle consulted the little clock in the taskbar: still a couple hours until shift change. He didn't feel like dealing with the tape rotation and a quick glance at the bandwidth charts told him everything was fine. He browsed to CNN's website to see what was going on in the world.

No changes since this morning. He pondered where else he could surf.

A thought struck him. He knew that his browser went through a proxy and a content filter monitored by the administration, but he wondered how restrictive they would get. He surfed to a hack site he once used to test the web sites he'd created at Anderson for vulnerabilities. He downloaded a couple of packet sniffers—programs capable of tracing information packets traveling through the network and breaking them down to their component parts, often including the data they carried. With luck, Big Brother only filtered porn and similar Acceptable Use Policy violations. If not and they had a beef with what he was doing, he would just tell them he took it upon himself to do some security testing. No big deal.

He looked over his cubicle walls to make sure Keith and Bob weren't paying any attention to him, then started the installation. He clicked his way through a few screens, pausing once to change the install directory to one buried deep in the WINNT\System32 directory where nobody would ever look. The installer then took off on its own, placing its files and making appropriate registry tweaks.

A question window popped up. Do you want to replace grdnwndp.dll last modified 8/13/1998 with grdnwndp.dll last modified 4/13/2004? He clicked "Yes" out of habit and the installer rolled on.

"Oh, shit!" he gasped, and sat up in his chair. What had he replaced? Some .dll file or another, but already the rest of the file name escaped his memory. Was it important? With all this customized software, it was hard to be sure.

But then again, it was only a .dll file. He wasn't quite sure what .dll's did other than serve as reference files for most Windows programs. The system had thousands of them installed. And this particular .dll file was still *there*, just a little … different. He could restore his whole workstation from backup if he had to and have it right back to normal.

His computer chimed at him. He looked down to find an error message staring him in the face. "Calculation Error. Restart?" Beneath it were simple Yes and No buttons. Neither Bob nor Keith had told him about what to do should this happen; during training they were adamant that all the binary calculations ran with no errors before submission. He looked over his cubicle walls to see if they were around. They were both absent. He sat back down, looked at the screen and thought he should wait until one of them came back, but then he saw his queue was getting pretty full. Restarting would be a snap—it was just starting over. He shrugged and clicked Yes. The progress meter flickered, then returned to its original, all red state. The green bar dropped back to 1%.

Lunch time approached, and Bob and Keith still hadn't returned. He figured they must be taking care of a project, so he locked his workstation, picked up his black satchel, and left the office. He headed for Round Table Pizza off Jamboree Road. The rear of the restaurant would provide some privacy for him to read more of *The Golden Bough* and take some notes, as well as jot down his findings from today.

His lunch consisted of a personal deep-dish pizza with pepperoni and black olives, a large coke, and a lesson on rituals of the ancient Celtics, numerology, and the Kabbalah. It was fascinating stuff; he had no idea what it had to do with KDS, but at this point he didn't care. The Druids for example—anthropologists still argued over the significance of Stonehenge. Frazier opined that the stone monuments of Stonehenge served a higher purpose; that their specific shape and layout was all according to strict mathematical formulas that worked in conjunction with the sun and position of the stars. Rituals had been performed at this site at specific times— most historians and anthropologists weren't entirely sure of the purpose of those rituals yet, but the popular theory was that they came from the rites of a sort of fertility cult.

Lyle pondered this as he washed down the last bite of pizza with Coke, and he recalled a story he'd heard last year about another recent theory being bantered among those who studied

Stonehenge—that the shape of the monuments was said to emulate the sexual organs of a woman.

In other words, nobody knows shit, Lyle thought. He flipped through the book again, momentarily distracted as he turned the pages. One photo from the book showed ancient runes etched in clay; another picture showed symbols carved into the rocky wall of a South American mountain, their markings resembling numbers more than they did letters. A reference to the Kabbalah caught his eye, and he held the book open at that page.

The Kabbalists were responsible for modern day Numerology. Kabbalists were a sect devoted to the mystical side of Judaism, but included some elements of Christian and Islamic thought. They were influential from the 12th Century in Southern France, Spain, and Portugal. The belief that numbers had magical meaning went back even further, even to the Babylonians and ancient Egyptians. The use of numbers in religious and magical rituals continued to grow and was still widely held in modern times.

Could that be what Carl was talking about? He supposed the calculations could just as easily be related to numerology as financial forecasts or DNA decoding, but for what purpose? Maybe Carl had lost his mind, or the meth-induced hallucinations had finally caught up with him.

Lyle sat back and allowed the waitress to remove his empty plate and dirty utensils. So far, according to what he'd read, primitive man was one superstitious motherfucker. Every position of the stars was significant; rituals were worked, prayers uttered, potions brewed, all in accordance with the local population's fears and beliefs. The shamans held tremendous power and were considered the village's wisest men.

Language and mathematics worked hand in hand for them. They developed complex systems of religious beliefs, and supposedly harnessed the laws of nature to control the forces that came like a breath of wind in the night or to dispel an angry fire threatening the crops. Oral stories and myths became commonplace, an attempt to explain to the villagers how things worked; a way to help them make sense of the inexplicable.

Lyle paid and left, feeling more than a little dejected. He knew he had to be patient, that he had to keep reading and studying and it would all fall into place. Meanwhile, he had to be observant yet subtle about it at work.

Keith and Bob were back at their desks when he returned. He nodded to Bob, then took his seat and checked on his workstation. The calculation was just about finished. He made sure Bob and Keith were lost in their own work, then launched one of the packet sniffers he had downloaded. The calculation finished and he let the sniffer run while transferring the files.

Unfortunately, it proved useless. Most of the traffic he intercepted was completely unintelligible to him and the rest appeared to be encrypted. He gave up and closed the sniffer, then deleted the files. For all the skill he had with cryptography, they could have used a plastic spy ring out of a Cracker Jack box and he wouldn't have cracked it. He started the next calculation.

Having caught up with most of his other work, he surfed around the KDS intranet to kill time. He browsed through the company directory, viewing pictures of various staff members and their titles: Systems Administrator, Software Administrator, Database Administrator, Web Developer, Unix Programmer … the list went on. He found it hard to believe that everybody at the company devoted a portion of their day to running the binary file calculations. What purpose could that serve?

And most important, assuming Carl was right, how the hell did KDS really make their money?

At three thirty he started surfing some of the public relations sites he'd found a few nights ago that carried stories on KDS. They were all written in that same bland hyper-prose, loaded with marketing buzz words and bullshit. "KDS is the leading developer of specialized software and networking for the international medical community" was the most popular refrain. And while he read paragraphs describing some of the state-of-the-art hardware systems the company employed in carrying out their functions, not one article mentioned a positive result of the company's efforts.

Lyle sat back in his cube, his mind racing. When he worked at Anderson, they did some consulting work for Sutter Medical Group. The literature and articles they wrote about Sutter all touched on something the company actually *did*, validating their existence and promoting their product. Two years ago, Sutter contracted with a Canadian physician who'd developed a groundbreaking new maxillofacial surgical procedure that corrected a rare birth defect preventing a ten-year-old girl from smiling. Sutter paid for the expensive procedure, which most HMOs would have refused to do, and the resulting PR gave the public a warm fuzzy and proof that not all big companies were about greed.

There had been dozens of similar cases during Lyle's employment at Anderson, and he recalled similar anecdotes from another job he'd held during college, working for Floyd's Aluminum. Their literature had been just as bland as KDS's, but at least their website and brochures contained photos of their product, both on display and in use, proof that their product was doing *something*, however small, to enrich the lives of its customers.

KDS, meanwhile, didn't even hint at an end result.

Lyle glanced at the clock on his monitor and realized it was almost time to go home. The calculation meter reached 100% at last and he started a new one before packing up his satchel.

"Hey," Bob whispered behind him. Lyle turned around and Bob waved him over. "Wait for me by your car, okay?"

"What, you finally ready to talk?"

"Shh! Keep your voice down. Just be there, alright?"

"Sure."

His relief arrived a short time later and he left the room with a nod to Bob. Outside in the warm summer air, he loosened his tie and made his way out to the car. The interior was awfully hot, so he started the engine, cranked up the air conditioning, and waited outside while the engine ran.

A few minutes later Bob came scurrying down the sidewalk. His eyes darted left and right as he approached and sweat darkened the armpits of his pale-blue, collared shirt. He stopped by the Saturn's headlight, pulled a handkerchief out of his pocket, and dabbed it across his forehead as he furtively looked around.

"So, what's up?" Lyle asked.

"You know, Lyle, you really need to be more careful. Anita's got her eye on you."

"What do you mean?"

"Take today, for instance. What time is it? Four oh five? Four ten? And you're already out the door!"

"Yeah … Quitting time's at four."

"Man, I haven't been out of here before six in weeks!"

"*Six?* Are you crazy? Don't you have a family?"

"Yeah, but they understand. They know the cost."

Lyle couldn't believe what he was hearing. "Okay, why the hell is everybody so secretive around here? What's the deal with these number crunches we're running manually? A monkey could do what we're doing in there! Shit, *one guy* could take care of it all with a simple script!"

Bob paled, his eyes wide. "That's not even funny."

"Why? Afraid they'll lay us all off? That you'll lose your overtime?"

"No! That's not it at all! Don't you get it? We need perfect uptime! Not ninety-nine percent, not five nines, but absolute one hundred percent! If we fall behind even the slightest bit, the consequences will be dire!"

"Enough with the mystery. You tell me what the deal is or I call in sick tomorrow."

"You wouldn't dare," Bob said, taking the bluff.

"Try me."

Bob drew in a deep breath. More dabbing at his forehead.

"Fine," Lyle said. "See ya in a few days." He put a hand on the door handle to the car and lifted it.

"All right! Just, please, hear me out to the end. Okay?"

Lyle released the handle and bumped the door shut with his hip. "I'm listening."

Bob paused while a fine-legged blonde woman in a red power suit walked by. She gave them a funny look and a curt nod, but didn't stop. Bob watched her go and Lyle admired the sway of her hips for a second.

"The Plague of Athens," Bob said.

Lyle blinked, tearing his eyes away from the woman and bringing them back to Bob's wide, nervous stare.

"Say what?"

"During the Plague of Athens, smallpox wiped out a large portion of the population. A group of seers took steps to be sure it never happened again. Flash-forward to the Dark Ages. A small order of monks is slaughtered by pagans and their monastery is burned to the ground. The Black Plague sweeps through Europe, killing a third of the population in five years, and it takes the combined efforts of the sages and shaman of cultures around the world to keep it from spreading. Several more years pass before the alchemists can get it under control."

"Okay," Lyle began, not seeing where this was going. "I took World History in college too, but—"

"Mexico, the 1600s," Bob continued, ignoring him. "Conquistadors execute a Native American priest in front of his people and a disease called cocoliztli decimates the population."

"You're not making any sense."

"Be quiet!" Bob looked nervous now. "Russia, 1918-1921. The strife of the Russian Revolution and the deaths of the tsars result in a typhus outbreak. The death rate is over ten percent. Around the same time in the United States, experiments with Babbage's Difference Engine go horribly wrong. The Influenza Pandemic kills a fifth of the *world's* population due to American arrogance."

"What the hell are you talking about?"

Bob gave an exasperated sigh. "Don't you get it, Lyle? Haven't you ever wondered why the world's population surged so suddenly since 1945? Because we've managed to keep Mother Nature in check! We're using the magic of our age—*technology*—to battle disease!"

Lyle chuckled. "Come on, pull the other one. Next you'll tell me this is how AIDS started."

"It is! In 1979 two technicians debate over an upgrade to Unix. The company goes one way, and one of the techs tries to make his partner look bad with a little creative sabotage. Boom, AIDS."

"Bullshit."

"Need more? An error with some punch cards in '68 creates bad output. Think Florida's hanging chads were a mess? This one caused a nasty dysentery outbreak in Central America, killing twenty thousand people."

"You're telling me technological mistakes caused all that?"

"Almost. African genocide and the murder of some tribal witch doctors brought back Trypanosomiasis, or the Sleeping Sickness."

"You know what, Bob? You're nuts."

"No, he's not." They both flinched and turned to see Keith standing in front of the Saturn. He had his hands in his pockets and a cigarette dangling from his lips. "You'd do well to listen to him, Lyle. Or, even better, to get your ass back inside and bring up your piss-poor productivity."

"Or what? They'll fire me?"

Keith shrugged.

"Maybe," Bob advised him.

Lyle stared at them. It was bullshit. All of it. It had to be.

Then the numerology he had been studying all sprang to mind, as well as Carl's sudden desertion and insistence on Lyle's quitting. His knees felt weak, and he leaned against his car, hoping Bob and Keith wouldn't notice.

"Why didn't anyone tell me this before?"

"You've only been here three weeks," Keith said. "Technology assisting alchemists around the world with the data necessary to keep humanity in the chips isn't exactly something people blindly accept. The company has to make sure you can be trusted and that you'll be reliable."

Lyle rolled his eyes. "I get it. A prank on the new guy, right? You're just fucking with me."

"I wish that were true," Keith said. "Did you tell him about our last Code Orange?"

Bob shook his head.

"Code Orange?" Lyle asked, looking at Bob. "What's that?"

"Code Orange is our mid-level alert," Keith explained. He took a drag on his cigarette casually. "Similar to the terrorist alerts the government initiated following 9/11. Yellow is very low risk, orange is mid-level. Red is serious and black is our highest alert. Believe it or not, most of the fuckups that happen in our little industry result in yellow or orange. It's rare that we get a red, and we've never gotten to black, thank God."

"So, what happened?" Lyle asked, still not believing this bullshit but wanting to hear the rest of it. He glanced at Bob, who refused to meet his gaze.

"Last year we had a guy in your position who was a good fit," Keith continued. "Kind of a geek, but very intelligent. He had no family to speak of, so he liked staying late and hanging out to get extra work done. He even had aspirations to climb the ladder, maybe help find a better way to crunch the numbers. Then they told him what the numbers did. He said he believed it, but in the end, he just had to be sure. So, he hacked a server and deleted one of the files out of the first queue. The Code Orange went out fifteen minutes later."

"And?"

"The CDC and the World Health Organization went on alert. By the end of the week the first SARS cases were being reported."

"SARS?"

Keith nodded.

"You know what?" Lyle snapped, his fear taking over now. "I've heard enough. Fuck you both, and good night. I'm out of here." He yanked the car door open and climbed inside.

Bob grabbed his door and started to say something, but Lyle ripped it out of his grip and cranked up the radio. Keith seemed to be saying, "Let him go" as he motioned for Bob to back off. Lyle shifted hard and backed out of his space, then jammed on the gas and headed for the exit.

"Fucking SARS," he muttered. "Who do they think they're fooling?"

Nevertheless, numerology and that overwritten .dll file nagged at the back of his mind all the way home.

CHAPTER THIRTEEN

The first thing Lyle did when he got home was pull *The Golden Bough* out of his bag and sit down at the dining room table. He'd driven all the way home with a lead foot and twice he'd had to pull over to calm his nerves. The more he thought about what Bob and Keith told him, the more scared he got. And with Carl jumping ship so suddenly, begging him to quit his job, it had to add up.

Lyle paged through the book, trying to find references to priests or magicians aiding in warding off disease, but he couldn't find anything. There were chapters about wood spirits and satyrs, soothsaying and turning lead into gold, references to a deity known as Hanbi or Hanpa, and entities known as the Watchers and the Mazzikim, but none of these helped. He found passages about curing individual disease, but nothing about warding it off en-masse.

He soon became too agitated to concentrate. He flipped through to the index, found dozens of entries on magic being used to ward off storms, disease and invading armies, and as he flipped to the appropriate page to begin his reading further, his cell phone rang.

Lyle scooped it up quickly. "Yeah?"

"Lyle?" It was Carl.

"Carl! Listen, I talked to some of the guys at work and they told me some crazy shit about KDS crunching numbers to help magicians and priests in—"

"It's too late, Lyle, they're on to me." Carl's voice was strangled and he coughed weakly.

A stab of fear went through Lyle's belly. "You okay?"

Harsh breathing on the other end. Lyle could hear traffic in the background. "Damn … this motherfucker hurts."

"Are you sick?" *Oh Jesus, don't let the bad .dll file be the thing that fucks things up!*

"Not sick," Carl managed, his breath a wheeze. "The minute I stepped in this phone booth to call you ..." He paused, seeming to struggle with his speech. "... I was shot."

"What?"

"Leave ..." Carl said, his voice rough, fading. "Pack up ... leave now ..." There was a thump on the other end and a series of cracking sounds, then the background noise of the traffic from wherever it was Carl had called from.

"Carl! *Carl!*"

There was more noise, an excited voice. Lyle kept shouting Carl's name and he thought he heard another voice in the background, distinctly male, say, "Jesus, man, there's blood all over this guy! *Hey! Hey, somebody call an ambulance!*"

Lyle yelled into the phone and a moment later he heard somebody's voice on the other end. "You talking to this guy?"

"His name's Carl," Lyle yelled, clearly panicked now. "He's just been shot!"

"I'm hanging up and calling an ambulance," the man said and then the line went dead.

CHAPTER FOURTEEN

He heard Melissa's car pull into the driveway a few minutes later, and he ran out to greet her.

"Hi, hon!" she called cheerfully, her features changing as she saw the look on his face. "What's wrong?"

"Carl's been shot," he told her. "He just called and passed out as I was talking to him."

"Oh my God, that's terrible! Have you heard anything else? Do you know where he was calling from?"

"I have no idea," Lyle said, trying to control his voice. He took Gabriel from her and carried him into the house while she carried her purse and bags.

Had it really been KDS that shot him? Did they want to keep him quiet that badly? Would they do the same thing to him and his family? Lyle didn't want to take that chance, but he didn't know how to bring the subject up to Melissa. There was no way she'd believe him.

"Maybe you should star sixty-nine the call," Melissa said. "Find out where it came from."

"I'm sure the police will trace the call he made through the phone company." Lyle set Gabriel on the floor and the boy quickly busied himself with a nearby picture book.

The next hour passed in a haze. Lyle wasn't hungry and Melissa gave him his space. He paced the kitchen, then sat in the living room and stared blindly at the TV. He felt restless and helpless. He didn't know whether to bolt out of the house and just start driving, escape California entirely with his family, or sit down and wait it out.

He felt sure Anita knew he'd finally caught on to their secret. He wondered if she'd prepped Bob and Keith for the little discussion they had today. Why else would they tell him so quickly? Or cooperate so suddenly? She had to have known Carl was a loose cannon, and likely knew he'd given Lyle subtle hints about what was going on. Surely, she would want to protect her investment in Lyle, which would make sense in getting Bob and Keith to spill the beans on him today. Just give him the whole story right up front. If he accepts it, fine, they bring him fully into the fold. If he doesn't, if he thinks it's bullshit or that it's a prank, maybe they can keep the wool pulled over his eyes for a little longer until he's entrenched enough to be shown the whole truth.

But if he reacts in the wrong way ...

Lyle fidgeted on the sofa. That's what had him so worried—what did Anita really know? What did she think about him? If he only knew that, if he could only be completely honest with her, he'd feel a lot better.

The phone rang, shaking him from his thoughts. Melissa answered and passed it on to him, her expression grave. It was a San Francisco Homicide detective who confirmed Lyle's worst feeling: Carl Sanders was dead.

Lyle couldn't concentrate as the detective tried to ask him questions. "Listen, I can't talk right now," he said. "I'm really upset. Can I ... can we talk some other time?"

"Sure," the detective said, his tone indifferent. He rattled off a number that Lyle jotted down on a notepad and hung up.

Melissa stood in the doorway to the kitchen. Tears filled her eyes. "I'm so sorry, Lyle!"

She came to him and he held her, feeling overwhelmed by the loss and the fear that still raced through him. He was so close to telling Melissa the whole story then, everything from the beginning, but that small voice of reason whispered to him. *Give it one more day. Go in tomorrow morning and talk to Anita. You need this job. You can't just up and quit. Talk to Anita, lay it on the line with her. Five to one says that will gain you a positive outlook on everything. It will provide you with a nice reality check. After you talk to the detective again, maybe you'll also learn more about Carl's homicide—for all you know he was killed in the crossfire of a gang shooting. And if Anita really does confirm what Carl, Bob, and Keith told you, well, you can cross that bridge when you get to it.*

"Everything will be okay," Melissa said.

The squeal of a toddler broke the din of dread that had settled over the house and Melissa and Lyle looked up to see that Gabriel had crawled into the living room. He sat down, chubby arms and legs stuck out in front of him. He sneezed once, smiled and giggled.

Despite everything, he laughed. Melissa laughed with him and for a time the dark pall was broken.

It did not return until later that evening as he lay in bed, and then it kept him up for most of the night. He kept trying to tell himself that the overwritten .dll file from this afternoon wouldn't be such a big deal.

CHAPTER FIFTEEN

Melissa was in a deep sleep when he gave up and got out of bed at four thirty. He'd dozed maybe an hour and there was no way he was getting back to sleep. He glanced at the clock. He could make it to work in under an hour, before the graveyard tech went home. He'd feel a lot better if he went in and assured himself that the overwritten file was no big deal. He went to the bathroom and brushed his teeth, washed his face and shaved quickly, then dressed silently.

He gently shook Melissa awake. "Hey, honey, I'm going in early this morning."

"Wha?" She coughed once, her eyes fluttering. "What happened?"

"I'm going in early. There's something I want to catch up on. I should be home early."

"Can you pick up the baby from daycare?"

"Sure, babe."

"'Kay." Melissa was already falling back to sleep.

Lyle tiptoed out of the bedroom, looked in on his sleeping son and noted the calm rise and fall of his chest, then left the house.

The lack of traffic on the 405 cut his trip from an hour to thirty minutes. Lyle drove into the KDS parking lot and pulled up to a spot close to the building. It was still dark outside, but it wouldn't be much longer. He'd go in, check with the graveyard tech, make sure things were okay.

He sat in the car for a moment, wondering how he was going to get through the rest of the day—the rest of the week—knowing what he knew. His leg itched and he scratched it absently, telling himself to just take things one step at a time. Go in, talk to the graveyard tech. If things were cool, no harm done. It would show he was concerned and he could use that as a springboard for his talk with Anita today, which he would insist on. He'd lay it all out for her, from Carl's insinuations to what Bob and Keith told him. If she continued to play dumb, he'd insist she call them in, but he had a good idea that she wouldn't do that. He knew there was something up, that there was some truth to everything he had learned this week and that he had to have it confirmed.

Then he could deal with it.

But first he had to believe. He had to know the truth.

He walked into the building, using his key card to get in the lobby, then headed down the hall to the control room. The nightshift guard nodded at him as he passed by; Lyle figured he would assure himself things were fine during his talk with the tech, then maybe he'd go to the cafeteria when it opened and have a nice, big breakfast and a lot of coffee. Then he'd return to his cube and start his day.

Heaving a sigh, Lyle inserted his key card in the slot to the door of the control room and let himself in.

A pair of techs stood at the rack of servers and there was a lot of activity in the cubicles, and a lot of people he didn't recognize. Some were on phones, others worked at the computers, and still more seemed to be standing around and waiting. Lyle saw Anita standing amidst the crowd and noticed she wore the same clothes he'd seen her in yesterday. His stomach dropped as if tossed down an elevator shaft. The techs turned to him and so did Anita. Her look of worry and fatigue quickly turned to anger.

"My office, *now!*" She stormed past him out of the control center and Lyle felt his legs go wobbly as he followed her.

"What's going on?" he asked, immediately hating the way his voice sounded.

She didn't say anything. Her heels made miniature thunderclaps on the tile as she stormed on down the hall. They rode the elevator in silence, she fuming and he shrinking into the corner. The door was hardly open when she stepped out of the elevator and walked toward her office. He followed at her heels.

She opened her office and stepped inside, then moved aside and waited for Lyle to enter. She slammed the door behind him. Hard.

"You left for home yesterday with a calculation file running," she snarled. "What the fuck were you thinking?"

Lyle scratched absently at his arm and he felt a persistent itch above his right knee; he resisted the urge to scratch it.

"Ted had just come in," he said. "He's the swing shift guy, I figured he would have seen—"

"You should have *told* him," Anita snapped, eyes smoldering. "Do you know how long it took that job to finish?"

"N-no."

"*Two hours*, Lyle."

"Sorry," was the best response he could come up with. Lyle wondered where this was going and what the big deal was. The itch in his leg got worse and he quickly scratched it.

Anita sighed and sat down. Lyle set down his satchel and took a seat in front of her desk.

She scratched her head, then coughed into her fist. "Alright, look. I'm sorry I snapped at you, but I've been here all night trying to figure out why the batch jobs are running so slow now. They're not supposed to run this slow. The one you kicked off before you left was the first one. You didn't see any of the ones you ran before that run that slow?"

"No. They ran fine all day."

"We traced the output logs. It looks like it started with your workstation, then spread to the others. Now it's across the entire network."

"You mean everyone's having the same problem?"

Anita nodded. She coughed again; her eyes looked red, tired. "Dave came in and did virus scans on all the servers, but didn't find anything. We did memory dumps, shut servers down and re-partitioned drives, defragmented drives, redirected network traffic, ran some new cables for more bandwidth … We just can't figure out where the problem is."

He almost asked her what the significance of the binaries and the backups were, but decided this may not be the best time. If he could do something to help, maybe it would help smooth things over.

Out on Technology Drive the wail of a siren screeched, becoming louder as it drove by. It then faded out in the other direction.

"So, it started on swing?" he asked.

"Yeah." She scratched the back of her neck and stretched. "We haven't had any alerts go out yet—nothing's really happened to warrant it. There've been no errors reported on the calculations, just the long delays." She paused, her hazel eyes appraising him. "Bob and Keith told you about the alerts, right?"

Lyle nodded. "Yeah, they did."

"So, you see how serious this is?"

He swallowed hard and nodded. "I think so."

So, it's real, he thought to himself.

Anita coughed again, twice. Lyle fidgeted in his seat. Watching her made his own throat feel dry, and his shoulders and arms started to itch worse; it felt a lot like the poison ivy rashes he'd picked up in the tenth grade, seeming to emanate from deep under his skin. He scratched his left shoulder vigorously.

"It gets worse," Anita said. "This morning the servers in New York slowed down and we're hearing now that they've slowed in Europe and Australia. The techs in those data centers are working at trying to pinpoint the problem, but so far nothing."

"What does this mean?"

"It means we have to find out why this is happening and fix it. Immediately. Then comes the problem of catching up."

He looked out the window of Anita's office and could already see the morning commute jamming up the 405. A set of flashing red lights ran up the southbound shoulder.

"Is there anything I can do?" Lyle asked.

"You can start by telling me if you have any idea what happened on your workstation that could have caused the problem."

"Nothing that I can think of offhand."

"Lyle, I can't stress to you enough how important this is. This is not the time to lie, even to cover your ass. There's a lot more at stake here than your job."

Lyle's breath hitched in his throat. "Is that a threat?"

"Let's just say I don't want you to underestimate the gravity of the situation."

Lyle's fingers tightened around the end of the armrest. Anita glared at him, and he held her gaze.

"Fine," she said after a moment. "Let's go down and see if anything's changed."

CHAPTER SIXTEEN

For the next three hours, Lyle listened carefully as Ted explained what he and his fellow nightshift techs had done to pinpoint the problem of the slow network. Lyle got a chance to look at his PC desktop and see if any changes had been made since he'd deleted the packet sniffer. Everything looked normal, and the overwritten .dll file was still out there on the server. He wondered if he could restore the older one from last night's tape backup and he briefly pondered this as Anita stood with Ted and one of the other night-shift guys.

It couldn't hurt. He stole a glance at the server, saw Anita standing in front of it with William and Ted, and quickly guessed that they would see him trying to restore something from last night's backup and would grow suspicious. This might lead to an investigation and his crime would be uncovered. He'd be fired for sure.

He sat in his cube, his stomach turning as he debated his options. The itch on his shoulder had spread and now most of his body itched. He scratched, wondering if it was a nervous reaction due to his emotions going haywire. His mouth felt dry, his head ached, and he felt a tickle at the back of his throat. That could be due to the dry climate of the control room. He scratched his knee. The minute Anita and the other techs left he would eject the tape from the server, rush to the vault for the previous day's tape and swap them. He could run the restore from his workstation, replacing his entire system directory just to be safe, and everything would be fine.

He never got the chance. Anita's cell phone rang, and he watched as she picked it up and spoke quietly.

"You're shitting me!" Anita said, casting a smoldering glance at

Lyle. His heart sank. Her eyes remained riveted on him until she hung up and tucked the phone into her pocket.

"Ted, Bill," she said, still glaring at him. "Grab Lyle."

The two men rushed him. He leaped out of his chair and dashed out of his cube, but one of them tackled him from behind. His forehead struck the door, stunning him momentarily. The two of them quickly overpowered him and hauled him to his feet.

Anita stepped up to him and crossed her arms.

Lyle struggled. "What the hell is this?"

"Congratulations, Mr. Harrison." Anita scowled. "You've just caused our first Code Black."

CHAPTER SEVENTEEN

He fought Ted and Bill as they dragged him toward the tape vault. Bill kidney-punched him, twice, taking the fight out of him. He collapsed to his knees in the vault and they slammed the heavy door behind them. Lyle tried to open it, throwing his shoulder into it when the knob would not turn, but finally gave up. The damn thing was probably engineered to stay up through all but the worst of California quakes.

He paced the room, thinking about Carl and his family. He wondered if he'd told the truth, maybe they wouldn't have done this to him. Then again, if he admitted to trying to hack the binaries, how pissed would they be? And now they probably knew about that anyway.

"Let me out of here!" he shouted at the door, for all the good it would do. He poured his fury into it, kicking and punching and throwing himself into it. It hardly rattled, and after a moment he had trouble drawing breath. He realized he was hyperventilating.

He sat down on a shipping crate and bowed his head between his knees to calm his breathing.

Code Black.

Oh God, what have I done?

Outside the vault, he heard frantic voices. He couldn't tell what was being said, but the tone of the voices certainly didn't indicate good news.

He forced himself to think as his breathing calmed. The vault was a small room, twelve by six, mostly containing locking cabinets for tape storage. A rack on one wall served as a sort of staging area for the current rotation of tapes. Lyle stepped up to it and searched for the tape from two nights ago. It looked like the D Server tape, which would contain his workstation, had been rotated out for examination. A simple compare operation would show them exactly what files he had changed, and probably even tell them what he had downloaded.

The activity continued outside. He caught snatches of conversation, most of it frenzied and worried. His stomach did a slow roll as he reached down absently to scratch his ankle. If Bob and Keith were right and SARS was just a Code Orange, then what would a Code Black bring about? How fast would it spread? How devastating would it be?

Time passed, but Lyle had no way of knowing how long. He thought of calling the police or the feds or someone, but his cell phone was still well out of reach in his satchel under his desk. After a while he had to piss, and thought about taking a leak in the corner just for spite.

Part of him still couldn't believe what was happening. It was lunacy to think that the very fabric of man's existence, the barrier that protected humans from total devastation from the forces of nature, were the combined efforts of shaman, priests, magicians, and *computers*. He always thought the advancement of medicine was to cure disease and prolong life. Following the discovery of penicillin and things like the smallpox and polio vaccines, medical research took off. And look what they were doing to improve the health and lives of people afflicted with HIV and AIDS. Just twenty years ago AIDS victims dropped like flies. Now it was believed they could live out an average expected lifespan with HIV and not develop full-blown AIDS so long as they followed a strict regimen of therapeutic drugs designed to ward off the disease.

Even if KDS provided the calculations necessary to assist magicians and seers around the world in keeping catastrophic illness and pandemics at bay, Lyle found it hard to believe that the conspiracy had never been uncovered. In all his research on KDS, not once did he find even a subtle hint or rumor of what the company really did. Surely someone out there, given all the conspiracy nuts around the world, would have come up with something.

And why all the secrecy? One would think KDS would be lauded worldwide for its efforts.

He recalled KDS had been founded in 1938, and by 1957 they had offices on every continent. That would dovetail with the emergence of supercomputers, and he supposed their power had grown in the early days of the Internet. He supposed on some level KDS must put out a product or service to generate a profit to keep it running, but if so, it surely wasn't advertised. And if they had no such product, the question becomes who funds the operation? Lyle certainly wasn't the only one generating a comfortable living income from the company, and he was at the bottom of the food chain.

So, they had to be funded by something big, but what? He couldn't see American taxes funding the whole thing, especially with branches around the world. The UN? No way. They couldn't even agree on the color of the sky.

Bob had mentioned the Black Plague as one of the first major events that the supposed mystics of the time had to combat. He also seemed to suggest those mystics around the world had united, had organized against a common threat. Perhaps that same unifying force provided the same guidance today? He wished he had paid more attention in history class.

The various European kingdoms certainly had power and colonies around the world. That was also an important time for Christianity and the various popes, who had power throughout Europe. They had overtly resisted science, denouncing men like Galileo and Copernicus and their discoveries. Then, of course, were the tales of rare manuscripts kept under lock and key in the bowels of the Vatican, presumably their key to power all over the world. Some said those manuscripts dated back before time—at least the time most people were familiar with and learned about in school—and encompassed records of lost civilizations like Atlantis.

Add into that the conquering of South America by the Spaniards, and whatever they may have brought back to the Old World, and it fit with Bob's story of the slaughter of the Aztec priests and the disease that later decimated their population. Lyle's imagination raced. Wasn't it possible that a conquistador or Spanish missionary made the connection and reported it back to Church officials? And that through hundreds of years of trial and error the administrative functions of various religious organizations had banded together and privately funded KDS? Figure all the collection plates across America during mass every Sunday, plus various other charitable contributions, and there'd be plenty of money to go around.

The more ridiculous it sounded, the more it started to make sense. Despite their position on demonic possession in modern times, the Catholic Church still had a secret panel that investigated such claims. Various Christian denominations also publicly debunked long-held superstitions once held by their believers while secretly practicing such rites: speaking in tongues, faith healing, and practicing mild forms of what hardline Evangelical Christians would call witchcraft. Suppose a very select few were still practicing magical rituals that helped keep the forces of disease and pestilence at bay?

He stopped before he could spook himself further. Historical research could come later. Right now, he just wanted out. The voices outside began to subside and he tried the door again. No joy. Surely Bob or Keith had arrived by now. Maybe they would convince someone to let him out.

Yeah, fat chance. They would follow Anita's word just like the rest of the goons around here. So, he waited. The voices came and went, and at least once a voice boomed over the PA calling for someone to take a phone call.

Finally, footsteps approached the door. The vault handle turned, and at last the door swung open. Lyle stood slowly as Bob peered in at him, his eyes wide with fear and fatigue.

Lyle felt relieved at first, then spotted the red blotches on Bob's face. Lyle's own chin itched and he absently scratched it.

"Don't do that!" Bob snapped. "It'll spread!"

Lyle glanced down at his hand and his heart leaped in his chest. The back of his hand was covered with the same red spots. "Bob, what's going on?"

"The shit is hitting the fan." A brief coughing fit interrupted him. "Look, nobody knows I'm down here. They're trying to blame all this on you, and everybody is up in Anita's office now talking to London. Whatever this is, it's spread everywhere!"

Lyle pushed past Bob and headed to his cube. "Where are the backup tapes? I can fix this."

"In the system, I think," Bob said. "The upper level techs imaged our hard drives and programmers are poring over every line of code they can get their hands on."

The control room door opened suddenly, and Anita stepped in. She looked sick, her face flushed and sweaty, her hair hanging in her eyes. Those familiar red blotches had spread across her face. When she saw Lyle, her face became a mixture of anger and hate.

"What the hell is he doing out, Bob?"

"I—" Bob began, his voice a nervous quaver.

"I'm calling security." Anita reached for her cell phone.

"Wait! Anita, I can fix this. I think I know what happened. We just have to restore the .dll file that got overwritten yesterday and—"

Anita ignored him. She nodded at Bob. "Grab him. Don't let him near the servers!"

Bob hesitated, scratching his chest.

Lyle started for his workstation. If the tapes were still in the system, maybe all was not lost. One simple rollback, and maybe all of this would go away.

"Get the hell away from there! Haven't you done enough damage?" Anita ran toward them, one arm reaching for Lyle as the other held her phone to her ear. "God damn it, Bob! *Hold him!*"

Lyle turned and shoved Anita with both hands. She stumbled backward and her shoulders slammed into the opposite wall. She screamed into her cell phone. "I need somebody here *now!*"

Then he hit her. He'd never hit anybody in his life, especially not a woman, but he hit Anita right in the face. His closed fist slammed into her cheek just below her right eye with a beefy *smack*. The blow rocked her head back, and the back of her head struck the wall. She slid to the floor, her eyes glazed. Lyle felt a quick twinge of guilt that faded as quickly as it came.

He turned to Bob, who stood like a deer trapped in a semi's high beams. Bob looked down at Anita, then at Lyle, then back at Anita. He appeared to be torn between helping a friend and doing his job, but Lyle suspected either way, the shell-shocked man would be of little help.

"Fine, just stay out of my way for a few minutes," Lyle said. He sat down and logged in to his workstation.

Anita groaned and sat up. An ugly red mark marred her cheek. "What do you think you're going to do? Don't you get it? It's already too late. We're in Code Black."

Lyle threw his keyboard to one side. "Why didn't someone tell me?" he demanded. "Why all the secrecy? I would never have done this had I known this was so important."

"Think about it," Anita said as she pushed herself to her feet. "You made one little mistake. Imagine what would have happened if someone tried to cause intentional damage. We'd probably be dead already."

"Security through obscurity? I don't buy it."

"No? Think of how many people would want to get their hands on this stuff if they knew it existed. We're practically sitting on the Holy Grail, Lyle. We'd have eternal life nuts and apocalypse whackos beating down our door every second of every day.

"Now, I'm telling you, step away from the computer and let our people do their job."

Lyle wondered if he would have to sock her again to shut her up when running footsteps thudded down the hall outside, and the door to the control room burst open. Anita pushed herself up to her feet.

Lyle recognized the security guard as the same one that had greeted him earlier. In the few hours since he'd arrived, the guard had broken out in dozens of red sores, some of which broke and oozed blood and yellow pus. His eyes looked yellow, disoriented. He glanced around the room quickly and saw Anita, who pointed at Lyle.

"*Get him!* Get this man away from our systems!"

The security guard rushed the cube. Lyle threw his second punch of the day, which plowed into the security guard's nose. Blood squirted from his nostrils and Lyle felt the wet squirt of the man's sores popping beneath his knuckles. The guard, already groggy from his illness, staggered back. Lyle grabbed his satchel, threw his shoulder into the guard and dashed out the door.

He ran straight out of the building and stormed through the parking lot. Breathless, he unlocked the door to the Saturn and threw his satchel on the passenger seat, then slid behind the wheel and started the car. He glanced up quickly and saw the guard and Anita running out of the building with several others in tow. Someone pointed in his direction, and the whole crowd turned toward him. He tried to calm his trembling hands as he pulled out and sped across the parking lot away from them.

It was just one bad file, he told himself. *How is this possible?*

His thoughts ran in continuous streams as he rushed the gate. The Saturn's grille crashed through the wooden gate. A broken piece cracked the windshield and spun away as he tore out of the parking lot. Lyle ducked instinctively but managed to keep the car going and tore down Technology Drive, ignoring the dazed expressions of morning commuters who looked at him with foggy expressions. He reached Jamboree Road and turned right against the light, ignoring the honking horns of other motorists as they braked to avoid hitting him. He gritted his teeth, hands tight on the steering wheel. He had to get home, had to reach Melissa before she left to take Gabriel to daycare.

The rashes erupted into boils that burned with the slightest brush of his clothing against his flesh.

CHAPTER EIGHTEEN

Lyle reached the 405 freeway when he realized he'd better slow down before a cop pulled him over. He couldn't afford that now.

He had to make it home. Had to make sure Melissa and Gabriel were okay, had to pack them up and then they had to make tracks and get out of town.

He observed the speed limit when he hit the northbound onramp. Traffic was still heavy, and he forced himself to calm down as the Saturn eased onto the freeway. He glanced around at the other morning commuters. Everything looked normal to him. As usual, there was roughly one person to every vehicle and they talked on cell phones or stared blandly into space. The perpetual look of the nine-to-five commuter. Nobody looked sick.

Everything looked normal.

Maybe it's okay, he thought, resisting the urge to rub his arm to alleviate the itching blisters.

Traffic crawled. He turned on the radio and got Howard Stern, who was trying to convince his female guest to take off her clothes.

He got his cell phone out of his satchel and pressed the speed dial for Melissa's cell, then cursed when a prerecorded message came on indicating her phone wasn't turned on. *Shit! Of all the times she forgets to turn her cell on, which was almost every goddamn day, she had to go and forget again today!*

He rubbed his arm, hoping the itching, burning blisters would go away.

They didn't.

He took another look around at his fellow commuters, trying to convince himself that everything was fine. Things looked normal; traffic was stop-and-go as usual, with people heading to work.

Engines rumbled, horns honked.

Sirens wailed.

Lyle listened to the sounds of the morning commute, trying to tell himself that the number of sirens he heard this morning was no more than usual. There seemed to be half a dozen of them or more, though, all coming from different directions. He glanced in his rearview mirrors, trying to see if anything came from behind him.

All was clear.

When he passed Talbert Boulevard he saw a Paramedic, siren blazing, followed by a fire engine heading north.

Lyle gripped the steering wheel, his heart racing. *Should I go to the hospital? Maybe I'm the only one infected out here; maybe it just hit KDS employees first.*

A sudden blast wailed from behind him. He glanced up in time to see two ambulances shoot past him, sirens wailing.

Ahead of him, a late-model Ford pulled to the side of the freeway and stopped.

Lyle passed it, stealing a glance at the driver. It was an older woman, slumped over the steering wheel. He didn't get a good look at her, but he could see that she was scratching her face.

Lyle watched the road ahead of him, debating where to go, where to get off. There was a hospital a few exits up, and already this section of the 405 was getting congested. He slowed down as traffic slowed. He heard the blare of more sirens as they passed below the intersection—Magnolia Boulevard—and he acknowledged now that it was extremely unusual to hear so many sirens on a weekday morning.

Lyle tried Melissa's cell phone again. It was still turned off.

Shit!

His chin itched and Lyle scratched furiously as the itch deepened. He made a quick decision as he crept along the 405. If he got off on Beach Boulevard and headed north he could get to the 22 and double back, then head toward Gabriel's daycare in Garden Grove. Melissa worked in Santa Ana, north of where they lived, and he could continue on a northeastern path until he arrived at their home in Tustin. He'd probably get to the daycare center just in time to intercept them. If not, he could pack up Gabriel, head by Melissa's office and get her, and they could go home or go to the hospital or do whatever they needed to do to get help. He had to make sure they were okay.

He checked for traffic coming up in the lane next to him, and when he saw an open spot he changed lanes. Twenty minutes later, the exit to Beach Boulevard came up. By then he had heard at least a dozen more sirens.

He turned on the radio and flipped through the stations: morning talk shows, scant music programs, news. Everything still seemed normal.

He monitored the news all the way to the exit, then took Beach Boulevard north to the 22 freeway heading east.

He saw more police cars.

More ambulances and paramedics.

And still no word on the news that anything was out of the ordinary.

Fighting back tears, he drove to Gabriel's daycare, his hands trembling on the steering wheel.

CHAPTER NINETEEN

His patience spent, Lyle gunned the accelerator and raced down the last three blocks to the daycare center and left the engine running as he dashed to the entrance. The front door banged off the wall as he burst inside. The children in the main room shrank away from him, and a parent standing at the check-in counter gave him the evil eye and hugged her child to her legs.

The skinny thirty-something owner looked surprised at his entrance. Her eyes darted to the sores on his forearm as he scratched vigorously. "Mr. Harrison … are you okay?"

"Has my wife showed up yet? Is Gabe here?" He craned his neck to survey the children already present.

"We haven't seen them yet. Is something wrong?"

"Shit!" He checked his watch. "It's after nine o'clock! They should be here by now."

"I don't know what to tell you. She hasn't called to cancel."

"God damn it!" He pulled his cell phone out of his pocket and punched in a series of numbers.

"Please don't speak that way in front of the children, sir."

He shot her an irritated look, then put the phone to his ear and ran back outside. The phone on the other end rang. Someone Lyle didn't recognize answered.

"Is Melissa there?"

"No, she isn't here yet." The voice was gruff, male. "Can I take a message?"

"Shit!" He thumbed the disconnect button and tossed the phone on the passenger seat as he climbed back into the Saturn.

He shifted to drive, then chewed his thumbnail for a moment. Where the hell could she be? She would have answered the phone—or at least called him back by now—if she was at home.

Maybe she can't answer the phone.

His best bet, he decided, was to follow her route between home and the daycare center and hope he ran into her along the way.

He drove east on Garden Grove Boulevard, trying to ignore the sirens he heard coming from all directions. As he drove he realized that his left hand felt numb. He shook it vigorously, but life did not return to it. Another symptom?

As he neared his home neighborhood, traffic picked up. Most of it came in the opposite direction, headed for the freeways or downtown. Strange. He hung a left on Pine Street and zipped past the local medical clinic.

A throng of cars packed the lot. He slowed down and looked over as he passed, and saw a tall man helping a dark-haired woman toward the door. A large red boil marred the side of her face.

Lyle hammered the accelerator. He tried to control his breathing, the sight of the woman with the large red boil imprinted in his vision.

He turned the corner onto Iroquois Street and hit the brakes upon spotting a throng of people halfway down the block. They mobbed an ambulance, reaching toward and pleading with the two paramedics in the cab. One woman held a small baby, the suppurating sores covering its body and arms visible even from a distance. The paramedics wore white facemasks and one of them futilely tried to shoo the people away from the vehicle. The ambulance's lights flashed and its siren barked periodically, and Lyle worried it had already taken a full load.

He straddled the curb to get around the crowd and a thin, beak-nosed man pressed himself against his window.

"Take me to the hospital!" the man pleaded. "My car was stolen! I'll pay you!"

Lyle gunned the engine and the man stumbled and fell away from the car, leaving pinkish streaks across the window. Lyle swallowed hard and hung a left on Cedar Terrace. Another block and he'd be home and still no sign of Melissa.

The radio suddenly blared with a loud beeping: *Beep beep beep beep beep!* "This is the Emergency Broadcast System. The following message is not a test. Repeat, the following is *not* a test."

He turned hard onto his own driveway and braked hard in the center. He climbed out of the car just as a grim-sounding man came on the radio to explain the situation. Lyle didn't need to hear it; he already knew what was happening.

The garage door was open but he saw no sign of Melissa's Taurus. It wasn't like her to leave without closing the door. He started toward the garage door when he spotted Melissa on the porch swing, rocking slowly and muttering something below her breath. Gabriel, disturbingly still and quiet, lay cradled in her arms. He ran over and jumped onto the porch.

"Melissa?" He went down on one knee in front of her. A polka-dot pattern of blisters ran up her right arm and the right side of her neck. Her left eye was swollen and raw.

She fixed him with her good eye. "Hi, baby."

"What are you doing out here?"

"Waiting for the ambulance."

He stared at Gabriel for several seconds before seeing the subtle rise of his chest as he took in a breath. A blister below his eye leaked fluid onto his mother's breast.

"They said they'd be here," she continued. "They said they'd come."

"Where's the car?"

"Somebody took it." Her face contorted into an expression of anguish and tears streamed down her cheeks. Sirens wailed in the distance and he thought he heard somebody screaming from several blocks over. "Oh, God, Lyle, our baby! I'm sorry! I'm so sorry!"

He clutched her tightly to his chest as his own tears started to flow. "It's not your fault, hon. Now come on, we have to get out of here."

She nodded and followed him back to the Saturn, holding Gabe close to her face and cooing and crying. He caught the words "unknown virus" on the radio before shutting it off completely. Melissa sat in the front seat and held Gabe across her chest. He didn't protest.

Under normal traffic conditions the drive to the hospital took fifteen minutes. Twenty minutes later he was still fighting his way through traffic with the rest of the crowd. The healthy ones were southbound, headed out of town with their windows rolled up and t-shirts, rags, and other makeshift masks tied over their noses and mouths. The rest, most covered with sores, fought their way north.

Twenty-five minutes later he noticed Melissa hadn't said anything for a while. Her head drooped forward, her chin resting on Gabe's shoulder. For a second he thought Gabe had stopped breathing, but then he detected a very slight rise and fall of his tiny chest. He could barely detect a faint stirring across the hair on the nape of Gabe's neck from Melissa's own shallow breathing.

Fresh tears distorted his vision. The ramp to the 405 lay just ahead. He chewed his lip, then wrenched the wheel right and nailed the back of a white Alero in the next lane. The driver pulled forward, giving him enough room to swing perpendicular and scrape the nose off a rust-spotted Astro Van before getting onto the shoulder and barreling for the ramp. He took it at high speed, nearly losing it and rolling off the edge of the cloverleaf turn.

Traffic choked the opposite lane. Several cars lay nose- or side-down in the median, some abandoned, some occupied by motionless bodies. Little to no traffic headed in his direction, though he and his like-minded companions often found themselves playing chicken with people coming the wrong direction.

Unlike his companions, however, he got off near the industrial park and headed for KDS. He could fix this. Just restore his workstation from a backup, crunch the numbers, and get through the queue and he'd be in good shape. He'd run ten workstations himself if he had to, but he'd fix this.

Technology and magic, computers and calculations. Just restore from backup and all will be well, a spell of his own to restore the natural order and correct his mistake.

Just restore from backup.

THE END

AFTERWORD

Yes, we are computer geeks.

One of us never intended to be a computer geek, while the other dived in headfirst upon realizing journalism didn't pay squat. We both have careers outside of publishing in the Information Technology sector that can be rewarding, fascinating, fun and, at times, infuriating and boring.

So, it was only natural that we mine our respective day jobs for the novella you just read. How we got here is a bit more complex.

Gonzalez had the basic seeds for this story in his commonplace book of story ideas for years when he approached Oliveri (after a suggestion from Brian Keene) about the possibility of collaborating on a short story for the *Borderlands 5* anthology. The reasoning was simple: we both wanted to write a story we could sell to the anthology, but neither of us had the time to work on a solo story—and we wanted to use our combined experience in IT to create something that was surreal and terrifying.

After tossing ideas back and forth we came up with an idea that we both liked. Then we set about to write it.

Problems showed up immediately.

The editors, Tom and Elizabeth Monteleone, wanted stories at around 5,000 words long. Anything longer, we'd have to query them on the idea before they gave the okay to submit it. With *Restore* pushing 7,000 words in its first draft, we figured it would be a long shot. This bad boy needed some work, and bad.

So, we revised it, trimming it down to 6,000 words. Still too long. So, we rewrote it again and finally got it to a length that we felt could squeak by.

What we came up with was great a great idea—but it was a

novella crammed into a short story. We discussed a few options, but it seemed a waste to put all that work into the story for *Borderlands* and not submit it, and despite the cramming problem we still felt we had a strong story. So, we fired it off and crossed our fingers.

Tom and Elizabeth passed on the story, saying they liked the general idea but they felt that, due to its overall theme, the piece would be better suited to a longer treatment. In other words, they felt it was a novella crammed into a short story.

Now that our initial feelings were validated, we set off to write it the way it should have been written: without tailoring it to a specific market. Of course, we had to make it exciting and dramatic, otherwise nobody would want it.

And wouldn't you know it … when it was finished, nobody wanted it anyway.

The problem, of course, was the goddamn length. Almost nobody publishes novellas anymore, and the few remaining professional magazine markets that still published them (*F&SF* and *Asimov's*) passed on this one. Neither of us were marquee brand name writers at the time, so specialty presses like CD Publications were out of the question. The few newer smaller presses that were starting up at the time this novella was finished (late 2003 into 2004) were still too brand new to consider publishing it, but both of the people who run them really liked it. So, into the drawer (or onto the thumb drive) this piece went.

Until Roy Robbins from Bad Moon Books stepped in and published it years later. Thanks, Roy! And now, a decade after that initial publication, it's back in print again from Crossroad Press (and includes a bonus short story set in the same world as the original novella). Thanks, Dave!

Technology has changed between the book's initial creation, its original printing, and this new edition, but the heart of the story remains the same, as it has throughout time.

It's been said in the business world that technology is king, and that's more so now in the early years of the twenty-first century than ever before. We are more dependent upon technology—and computers—for everything from keeping the power grids running, to storing sensitive banking and financial data, to ensuring the digital imaging equipment in hospitals displays the correct patient data for doctors to make solid medical decisions that could impact human lives.

It was with that in mind that the seeds of this story grew, and we asked ourselves: how could horror and technology mix (aside from murderous robots and psychotic computers, of course)? Instead of technology gone awry, we wondered how an ancient system—a magic or occult system—could evolve with the technology. How would massive computing power affect magic? A programmer's bag of tricks looks like magic to an outsider, so why not apply those same "spells" to the real world?

The next logical question became the story: what if one of those spells went wrong? It's a rare IT admin that hasn't seen a program or network fail due to one simple problem, like a corrupted file. Upload the wrong set of commands to the wrong router, and you can bring down huge segments of the Internet. In this case, our protagonist pokes around where he shouldn't and he overwrites a file. A file that previously had one function now performs another, and the program depending upon it fails.

Only instead of throwing off the personnel department's budgets, he crashes the planet.

We've both performed our fair share of panicked restore procedures, but a lost customer database pales in comparison to unleashing a deadly plague. Fortunately, the real world doesn't work that way.

Of course, distributed computing is now being used for cancer research and protein folding. What if someone tweaked a fold as a prank, submitted it back to the main repository, and that protein now disassembles muscle tissue instead of fighting a virus ...

Think it can't happen?

Think again.

Mike & Jesus
22 March, 2007 and 4 September, 2017

ALGORITHMS OF THE HEART

(A STORY FROM THE WORLD OF RESTORE FROM BACKUP)

By Mike Oliveri

These few lines of code would change his life. All Gary had to do was insert it into the subroutine and wait for love to blossom.

It's not that he couldn't find a woman, the problem was he couldn't *keep* a woman. The rigors of the job and its frequent odd hours made it difficult to maintain a relationship. The ladies he met just didn't have the patience or the stamina for it. He'd come close with Carly. She always said he was cute with his sandy blonde hair and requisite IT guy goatee, but eventually she, too, wore down and walked out on him.

That was a year ago. He knew going in this gig was as much lifestyle as career, and once he signed on all those dotted lines and worked his way through that miserable goddamned orientation program, he knew there was no going back to a normal life. For six months, he resigned himself to a lifetime of loneliness.

For the next six he worked on the code.

He kept it on an isolated server in his apartment, executing it over and over in a sandboxed simulation away from the prying eyes of his employers. He tweaked and massaged it, making sure there would be no runaway butterfly effect plunging everything into chaos. Last week, at last, he got it right. He committed the code to memory, then took the drives out of the server and smashed each of their platters to dust with a ball-peen hammer.

Now he stared at the terminal window. The cursor blinked at the end of the code. He'd already checked the syntax twice, then again, then once more.

His fingers hovered over the keyboard.

Click-click. Saved.

Shit. He could still erase it. The code wouldn't do a thing until he compiled it and fired it down to ops for execution. A few taps to erase those lines and nobody's the wiser.

But nothing would change, either. He closed the file, reset its timestamp to match the other files in the directory, then erased his command line history. He spent a half hour on busy work, checking files and tweaking code and prepping for the next upload. Business as usual.

A reminder chime *pinged* from his desktop: compile time.

He returned to the terminal window and chewed his lip for a second. Last chance.

"Just do it."

He typed out the compile commands, then stabbed the enter key with his forefinger.

Now he just had to wait.

Gary left his apartment in a fog. He'd tossed and turned through the night, half expecting explosions and sirens at any moment. During his shower and breakfast, he'd streamed morning talk radio, wondering if war had broken out or someone had been assassinated.

Nothing.

At least, nothing beyond the usual geopolitical shitshow. Maybe he'd gotten it right after all. Or if he *had* screwed something up, maybe it got lost in the rest of the chaos.

Win-win?

He hit the elevator button and sipped his coffee. Too weak. Today might be a good day to grab an espresso at the corner before he got on the train.

Ding. The elevator doors rattled open.

"Wait!" Down the hall, his neighbor Rachel hurried to lock her door. Her keys slipped from her hand and hit the floor with a thud. "Shit. Hold the elevator! Please?"

Gary wedged the side of his foot into the corner of the door. It gave him a light shove and gave up. Rachel stumbled down the hall, juggling her keys, a bulky black purse, and a green canvas messenger bag. Her keys hit the floor again.

"Damn it!"

The elevator door gave another little push, then made a series of indignant dings.

"Sorry, Gary!" She dropped her keys into her purse and slipped into the elevator. "Thanks so much. I'm running late."

"No problem." The elevator lurched toward the lobby. "How's Brady doing?"

"He's good. In San Francisco until tomorrow, actually. Say, now that I think about it, what are you doing tonight?"

"What?"

"I'm going to be rearranging the furniture in our place, but I'm not exactly built for that kind of work."

She gestured down the length of her body, and his eyes followed. She wasn't wrong. At all of 5'3" and on the thin side, she'd be hard pressed to shift a few couches around on her own. Today she wore a plain skirt with a plain blouse under an ugly sweater, all in contrast with a rather nice pair of heels. He tried to remember what she did. Office manager somewhere? More than a receptionist, anyway.

"So what do you say?" she asked. "I'll even spring for dinner!"

He didn't really want to, but she was probably just stubborn enough to try it on her own, and she and Brady were the only neighbors who weren't some combination of old, creepy, or annoying.

"Pleeeease?" She pressed her hands together and flashed a wide smile. It looked good on her, even with her hair tied up tight. Those bubblegum-pink glasses had to go, though.

"Alright, yeah. I'll be happy to help."

"Great! Seven o'clock okay?"

"Sure, I can do that."

"You're a lifesaver!" The elevator slowed to a stop, and she squeezed his arm. "Thank you thank you thank you! I've gotta get going, so I'll see you then. Bye!" And then she rushed out the door.

"I'm definitely going to need more coffee."

The office door opened, startling Gary awake. He spun in his chair to find Marty had just come in with a stranger.

"Oh, hey, Marty. Who's this?"

"Gary, this is Tom Damron," Marty said. "He's just finished orientation and is starting with us today. Tom, Gary."

"Nice to meet you." They shook hands. Tom was a tall and lanky guy, clean-shaven with his hair parted down one side. A man could almost cut a finger on the pleat in his black pants, and a little gold pin kept his blue tie neatly in place. Definitely eager to make a good impression. Give him a few months and it'll all change, after he realized most of the people on the floor will want to impress him instead.

"Likewise. Well, both of these desktops are available. Take your pick and make yourself comfortable."

"Thanks!" Tom picked the desktop near the window. The new guys always did. They think they'll like the view over the city, but then the sun stabs them in the eye all afternoon.

At least they had one of the nicer offices on the floor. Even sharing the workspace beat the cubicles the helpdesk and service drones had to put up with. There were four workstations, two each on opposite tables flanking the door. Gary and Marty had shared one for over a year now, and their notes and manuals and lunch detritus covered their space. They'd wedged a microwave and an old bookshelf stereo system between the desktops behind them.

Tom logged in, then tried to arrange his keyboard and mouse in the narrow space left between the microwave and the wall. Newbs never tried to make extra room on their first day.

Marty slumped into his chair. He was a big guy, though down thirty pounds already from the bariatric surgery the company had sprung for. He was damned good at his job, and they wanted to keep him around a while. Marty smacked his mouse to wake up his desktop, then his chubby fingers hammered out an absurdly long passphrase.

"You see the reports from last night's executions?" Marty asked.

Gary's heart thudded hard in his chest. Marty's main job was audit, comparing the results of last night's code runs against a mix of news sources, social media input streams, and field reports. His advice for course corrections usually made it into Gary's code.

"Uh, no," Gary said. "What do they say?"

"That's just it, they haven't showed up yet. I asked ops for them on the way up, and they said the reports weren't ready. No ETA."

"Huh. Another helpdesk snafu?"

"Probably. So!" Marty spun back around to face Tom. "Any questions? Hell, I bet you got a ton of 'em."

"Just trying to get acquainted. Some of this stuff looks a little different from what I expected."

"Ah, the orientation manuals are always behind the rollouts. They can't keep up with the changes, and we don't have time to walk them through it. But that's not the *big* question. Go on, you can ask."

They always asked. Always.

"Well …" Tom said.

Here it comes.

"Have you guys seen the Interface?"

Gary and Marty laughed. Every time.

"What?"

"Man, *nobody's* seen the Interface," Gary told him. "Except some guys in ops, maybe, but that little bit you get in orientation is all any of us know."

"We can't even tell you where it is," Marty added. "Hell, 'where' may not even be the right question."

"But surely we know how it works?" Tom asked. "What else would we be doing here?"

"Alright, look," Gary said. "Programming's just language. So is hocus pocus, and abra cadabra, and all that hokum in the Harry Potter books. It's all about communicating with the Interface, the ether, the other side, or whatever your religious, scientific, or cultural understanding of *it* is."

"So we're just putting that language together?"

"Exactly. Ops can only handle so much. It's all about efficiency. Think of the monks of old transcribing all that work. You think they only worked on Bibles all that time? Hell no. The printing press revolutionized a lot of the work, and now here we are in the digital age, taking it to the next level."

Tom nodded. "Why couldn't they put it that way in orientation?"

Again, Gary and Marty laughed.

"Because they're too caught up in procedure and making sure you're not going to fuck up," Gary said.

Then Marty turned abruptly serious. "But seriously, don't."

"Don't what?"

"Fuck up. That part of orientation, they definitely weren't kidding around. Just ask the last guy who sat in that chair."

Gary tried not to think about it.

Rachel crossed her arms. "I guess we can call it done."

Hopefully she meant it this time. Gary sat down at the kitchen table and wiped the sweat off his brow. She had him dragging two couches, a chair, and a heavy entertainment center to and fro for the last hour, and now he was pretty sure all they'd accomplished was to swap the couches. And did these people really need two sleeper sofas? They didn't even match! In fact, the whole place looked like the result of a second-hand-store shopping spree. It explained a lot about the way Rachel and Brady dressed, too.

"You think Brady will even notice?"

"He'd better."

"Yeah. Ugh. I really should have done some measuring first."

He'd suggested that an hour go. At least she'd ordered in from his favorite Thai place, and it was cute watching her fret over each move. She'd let her hair down and had been smart enough to change into flannel pants and a long-sleeved tee. Meanwhile, his dumb ass still wore his khakis and polo from work, both of which were now smeared with dust and sweat.

"Would you like a drink?" she asked.

"Sounds good."

She busied herself at the counter for a few moments, then came to the table with two rocks glasses. She'd drowned three black, cubical stones with amber liquid in each.

"What is this?"

"Bourbon," she said. "Brady loves the stuff. If we sample from a few different bottles, he'll never know we had any." She winked.

"Fair enough. Cheers."

"To friendship!" She clinked her glass against his.

The bourbon was sweet and strong, and it burned his throat all the way down. He coughed.

"Too strong?"

"No!" he said, gasping. "It's good, I just ... Wow."

"Brady only buys the good stuff. He and his friends can talk for hours about these things. That's why I didn't call any of them."

Gary took another sip, much smaller this time. At least the guy had good taste.

Rachel slammed back the rest of hers. "Want to try a different one? He's got a bottle with a horse and jockey on top. Looks like a grenade!"

"But I haven't finished this one, yet."

"Bottoms up, then! Let's go!"

He polished it off just as she walked over with the bottle, and she poured him two rather generous fingers.

So it went for the next hour, trading shots and sharing gripes about their daily grinds. Her frustrations with her family made him happy he had none to speak of. They killed a small bottle, and she laughed when he hoped it wasn't one of Brady's favorites.

Then she took off those silly pink glasses, and she looked a lot less childish. She had shining brown eyes, and a little upturn to her nose that he hadn't noticed before.

"What?" she asked.

Whoops, busted for staring. "I bet you can rock an evening gown."

One of her eyebrows went up.

"Sorry, I guess I said that out loud." He finished his glass, held it up. "Maybe too much of this."

She poured him another, told him, "I'll be right back." She slipped down the hall to the bedroom.

He sipped. Everything seemed fuzzy and swimmy, his face felt flush. Maybe he should go? He squinted at the clock, but it wouldn't stand still.

Rachel returned in a little black one-piece dress that hugged her curves. The sleeves hung down off her shoulders. The skirt revealed a colorful tattoo on her upper left thigh, something with birds and sparkles and a funky font he couldn't make out.

"Wow."

"I hoped you'd say that." She sat sideways in his lap and draped her arms around his neck.

"Whoa." He set his drink on the table. "I'm not sure this is a good idea, Rach."

"Why? You have problems with whiskey dick?"

"What? No, I—"

"Then shut up." She pressed her mouth to his.

She tasted like bourbon.

Gary woke up hot and sticky with a dull ache between his eyes.

Rachel. Shit. They laid beneath a blanket on the sofa, her naked body pressed against his in a spoon. He pulled his hand away from her breast and pushed the blanket down. The air felt cool on his chest and shoulder.

She mumbled something and snuggled deeper into the blanket, but she didn't wake.

Dammit, had his code done this? The kitchen fixtures cast their light into the living room. He eased himself up and over her, carefully rocked her onto her back, and lifted the blanket to her chin. He looked over at the clock: 3:34 a.m. At least he hadn't overslept. He gathered his clothes off the floor pulled on his pants in the kitchen. He wondered if he should clean up a little, especially the empty bottles.

No. His head felt like someone had dropped a brick on it, and just looking at the noodles and sauce near the sink made his stomach churn. Best just get the hell out. He fished his key out of his pocket and went to the door. He peered up and down the hall, then closed the door gently behind him. A couple more hours of sleep, a shower, and then he could figure things out.

"Dude, why did you even come in today?"

Gary blinked and rubbed his eyes. "Sorry, Marty."

"This is two days in a row. Get your shit together." Marty turned to Tom. "He's not always like this. I promise."

"Don't apologize for me!"

"I shouldn't have to!"

"Why are you riding me?" Had Marty seen something in the reports? Gary had been digging through files all morning, but there were no flags, no changes, no sign of any problems. And it's not like anyone had come to drag him out of here.

Marty glared at him. Tom half turned in his chair. Welcome to the job, kid.

"Seriously, go home, Gary. I don't know what you've been up to, but go home and squash it. Things are under control here."

"What does *that* mean?"

Marty sighed. "Seriously, dude?"

"Sorry. Sorry, you're right." Gary logged out and closed up his bag. Marty wasn't the one acting out of line. Marty would have his back, but only so far, and he didn't need to be under that microscope. "I just had another long night. I'll be fine."

Gary walked out and shut the door. Marty said something more to Tom, but he let it go. The cubicle drones paid him no mind. He checked his phone while he waited for the elevator. No message back from Rachel.

Ten minutes later on the train, he checked again. Still nothing. He wanted to send another message, but he didn't want to push it.

He shouldn't have sent that code. The sandbox had never failed him before, though, and it's not like he'd coded against a target. He just wanted to boost his luck a little. No harm, no foul. Hell, the ops guys probably did this kind of thing all the time, and who did they answer to?

The elevator took its sweet time getting to his floor. A little more coffee and some ibuprofen, and then he can log in remotely and take another look. He stopped in front of Rachel's door. Maybe she was home, and he could talk to her directly.

"It's too late now!" A man's voice, shouting behind the door.

Brady. Damn.

More back and forth between him and Rachel, too low to hear through the door. Not cool. Gary hurried to his apartment and locked the door behind him.

The remote access would probably set off a few alarms, but Gary had to find out what may have been changed. A pot of coffee and an hour of poring over code netted him nothing but another headache.

A knock at the door. Gary looked through the peephole and saw Rachel, no glasses, sporting a shiny red welt under her left eye. He whipped the door open.

"Are you okay? Did Brady do this?"

She waved him off as she walked past him. "Yeah. He's a dick, and I just need to be away from him for a little while."

"Shit, I'm so sorry. This is all my fault."

"Hey, *I* poured the bourbon. Can I get a bag of ice or something?"

"Of course." His hand shook while he found a Ziploc and filled it with ice cubes.

"Seriously, don't sweat it. This has been a long time coming. Well, not *this* this," she said, pointing to her eye. "Definitely the blow-up, though."

"I need to make a phone call. Will you be alright for a second?" He handed her the bag and she pressed it to her face.

"Sure, don't mind the girl with the face punched in."

"But—"

"I'm kidding, Gary. Go ahead."

"I … Yeah." He grabbed his phone and went into the bedroom, punched up Marty's number.

"Hi, Gary. What's up?"

"Hey, listen, did you ever get the run reports from the other night?"

"No, why?"

"I just need to know what happened with some of my code."

"That code never ran."

"What!? Why not?"

A pause on Marty's end. "They said there was a problem, but didn't say what. Tell me you didn't do something stupid."

If it never ran, then this wasn't his fault after all! But if they'd stopped it from running …

"Gary? You still there? Yesterday I got the order from ops to restore a big part of the code for that night. I assumed you got it, too."

"No, I didn't."

"Oh. Oh, fuck. You messed up, dude. I gotta go."

"Marty, wait!" The line went dead. Gary called back. One ring, then voicemail.

Someone pounded on the door.

"Fuck off, Brady!" Rachel shouted from the living room.

More pounding. "Open up!"

Gary ran into the living room. Ops only fixed these kinds of things one way. He didn't have a gun. Maybe he could make it to the kitchen before—

The door flew open and slammed into the wall. Brady rushed in, with his man bun and his ridiculous mustache and a long, fat knife in his hand.

"Brady, wait!" Rachel screamed.

Gary knew he'd never make the kitchen. Fucking ops, man. He watched the knife punch into his gut, right below his sternum. It knocked the wind out of him. Brady grabbed him by the shoulder, seemed to push him off the blade before stabbing him again, right between the ribs.

He couldn't breathe, and God, there was so much blood. He thought it would hurt more. Rachel screamed and screamed behind him. Brady pulled the knife out and let him fall to the floor.

He never felt the impact.

ABOUT THE AUTHORS

J. F. GONZALEZ was an author, editor, and noted genre historian whose works included PRIMITIVE, BULLY, THE CORPORATION, SCREAMING TO GET OUT, THEY, SHAPESHIFTER, RETREAT, OLD GHOSTS AND OTHER REVENANTS, BACK FROM THE DEAD and dozens more. His novel SURVIVOR is hailed by critics to be a seminal work of extreme horror. His collaborations with other authors include HERO and THE KILLINGS (both with Wrath James White), and the popular CLICKERS series (with Mark Williams and Brian Keene). To learn more about his legacy, visit jfgonzalez.org

MIKE OLIVERI is a Bram Stoker Award winning novelist and comic book writer whose works include THE PACK: WINTER KILL, THE PACK: LIE WITH THE DEAD, BRAVO FOUR, WEREWOLVES: CALL OF THE WILD, TO FIGHT WITH MONSTERS (co-written with Brian Keene), DEADLIEST OF THE SPECIES and many more. His short fiction has appeared in numerous anthologies and magazines. To learn more about him, visit mikeoliveri.com

Curious about other Crossroad Press books?
Stop by our site:
http://store.crossroadpress.com
We offer quality writing
in digital, audio, and print formats.

Enter the code FIRSTBOOK
to get 20% off your first order from our store!
Stop by today!

www.ingramcontent.com/pod-product-compliance
Lightning Source LLC
Chambersburg PA
CBHW071233170626
46809CB00008BA/3028